On the Line

Paul Coccia and Eric Walters

ORCA BOOK PUBLISHERS

Published in Canada and the United States in 2022 by Orca Book Publishers.
orcabook.com

Library and Archives Canada Cataloguing in Publication
Title: On the line / Paul Coccia and Eric Walters.
Names: Coccia, Paul, author. | Walters, Eric, 1957- author.
Identifiers: Canadiana (print) 20210183217 |
Canadiana (ebook) 20210183241 | ISBN 9781459827134 (softcover) |
ISBN 9781459827141 (PDF) | ISBN 9781459827158 (EPUB)
Classification: LCC PS8605.O243 O5 2022 | DDC jc813/.6—DC23

Library of Congress Control Number: 2021936142

Summary: In this novel for middle readers, thirteen-year-old basketball
star Jordan Ryker learns that his father is gay.

Orca Book Publishers is committed to reducing the consumption
of nonrenewable resources in the production of our books. We make
every effort to use materials that support a sustainable future.

Orca Book Publishers gratefully acknowledges the support for its publishing
programs provided by the following agencies: the Government of Canada,
the Canada Council for the Arts and the Province of British Columbia
through the BC Arts Council and the Book Publishing Tax Credit.

Cover artwork by braingraph/Shutterstock.com
Cover design by Rachel Page
Author photos by Shirley Coccia (Paul) and uncredited (Eric)

Printed and bound in Canada.

25 24 23 22 • 1 2 3 4

*For Eric, my friend and co-author, who shared the world
of this book with me but also freely gave and continues to
give the best of himself every second I know him.*
—P.C.

*To my dear friend Paul, one of the kindest, most generous
people I've ever had the good fortune to know.*
—E.W.

One

I rolled over and took the pillow away from my head. Wearing it like a gigantic earmuff wasn't working anyway. I could still hear them downstairs, fighting. My mom's voice was sharp and sometimes loud. My dad's voice seemed to vibrate throughout the house. I didn't so much hear it as *feel* it. There was no point in even pretending to sleep. I sat up and threw my feet over the edge of the bed.

It was their third "little disagreement"—as my mom called them—this week. And it was definitely the loudest and longest. It had started over whose turn it was to fill the gas tank on the truck and had begun simmering about thirty minutes before I headed up to my room. I'd seen enough fights to know it was only the warm-up act for the bigger fight to come. It was the reason I'd decided to go to bed early.

I'd excused myself and told them it was because I wanted a good night's rest before the tryouts the next morning for the school basketball team. I'd hoped that wouldn't be seen as just a good excuse but might actually calm things down so they wouldn't disturb me. Sometimes basketball was the only thing they both agreed on.

Of course, I didn't need any extra sleep to make the team. The coach had already told me I was going to be the starting power forward. It wasn't any sort of secret. I played for a "travel" team, just like my dad had when he was my age. I even played the same position. He had been my coach— formally and informally—since I'd first picked up a ball. I hoped that I could follow in his footsteps someday and land a basketball scholarship. I'd have to finish eighth grade and high school first though.

For now, all I wanted was for them to stop fighting and let me sleep. Or stop and let me lie in bed *trying* to get to sleep. It was so annoying that they were loud enough to keep me awake but not loud enough for me to hear what they were fighting about. I couldn't ask them to speak up, but I could make it easier for me to hear.

Without turning on a light, I quietly padded across the floor and along the hall. With each step I took, their voices got louder. At the top of the stairs, one landing and a turn away from the main floor, I could hear them clearly. I took a seat on the top step.

My mom's voice was emotional. My dad sounded calm. He always sounded calm no matter how angry or loud he got. That drove my mother crazy. She'd told me that. I figured my dad knew as well. But it wasn't like he was trying to do it deliberately—it was just who he was, calm and in control. It sometimes felt like there was a balancing act going on.

The calmer he got, the more emotional she got, and the more emotional she got, the calmer he got. When my dad got calm, I knew enough to be worried and keep clear of him until he… calmed up?

My mom had told me more than once that someday, when my wife and I fought, I would need to show emotion. I wished she'd stop saying things like that to me. I wasn't even sure I wanted to get married. I figured having a girlfriend was the first logical step before talking about a wife. Regardless, I wasn't planning on fighting with either one.

The fight downstairs had changed direction. It was about money now. Money had become *the* argument over the last few months. This one was specifically about a new chair my mom had bought for the den and some car parts my dad had purchased for his '69 Camaro. That car was his pride and joy. He'd been refurbishing it for longer than I could remember. It had been nothing more than a rusted-out junker with a seized engine when my dad had found it in his father's garage.

"That chair cost more than our first car," my dad said, his words crystal clear. "At least I could sell the Camaro for a lot of money. It's an investment."

"Who do you think you're kidding, calling it an investment? It's not like you're ever going to sell it. I'm starting to think you care more about that stupid old car than us."

My dad didn't respond right away. The silence made me feel the fighting even more. It was as if the whole house was vibrating and only we knew it. Mom had to have known she'd crossed a line. I was pretty sure she had done it deliberately, hoping to push him to say something more.

Finally he said, "We both know that's not true. Don't you think you're overreacting?"

"At least I'm reacting," my mom shot back. "Nothing gets past your defenses. Not my feelings. Not losing your job. Not the money."

I thought money fights might be going on in a lot of homes around here. The automobile plant where my dad worked was the biggest employer in the city, and it was closing down. The company had announced five months earlier that it would close in a year. Seven months left.

A lot of my friends had a parent or, even worse, two parents who worked at the plant. It was the only place my dad had ever worked. He'd started there during the summers when he was still in university because the money was good. Lots of kids of people working on the line had put themselves through school that way. After Dad graduated, he went back to the plant. It was supposed to be just for a while. The money kept him there. Well, that and my coming along. Not that he'd ever said anything to me, but I knew that hadn't been his plan. You don't get a college degree in American history because you're going to build cars. He had started on the line, become a supervisor and then a manager.

Usually being a manager made things better. Car plants had cycles. The workers on the factory floor would get laid off and then rehired. Managers didn't get laid off. In any event, a layoff was only temporary. People learned to budget money until they were rehired. Now nobody was going to be rehired. It was all just ending. And my dad wouldn't be a manager. He wouldn't be anything.

My dad had no tone whatsoever as he said, "I know what's coming. Don't you think I worry?"

My mom went unexpectedly calm too as she answered, "I'm not sure what you think. Do you know what it's like to live with someone and have to guess what's going on with them? What should I do, decipher it from which car parts you're spending money on this week?"

"Back to the money. We're not broke. We have enough for a while."

"How long do you think? I just bought Jordie new shoes for basketball. He's still growing." She sighed. "I did the numbers, the numbers I asked you to do with me. There's not as much there as you seem to think."

I instantly felt bad, even though I knew I couldn't control my growth. I hadn't needed to ask for the expensive basketball shoes either, though.

She started sobbing. Crying was the only thing worse than fighting. Not just for me, but for my dad. This was how fights often ended. Not settled but ended.

My mom got loud again, her voice now a strange combination of anger and garbled tears. I didn't think my dad knew what she was trying to say. I sure couldn't tell. I heard the front door close. Dad had left. I listened for what I was sure was going to come next—the full-throated rumbling of the Camaro as it started.

I scrambled to my feet and quietly moved back down the hall. I looked out at the driveway. I'd gotten there just in time to see him turn on the headlights. Even in the dark, I could see him in my head. My dad was six foot six, and he almost had to fold himself to get into the driver's seat. Once seated, I knew, he'd adjust the rear- and side-view mirrors, even though he was the only one who drove the Camaro. It was the last thing he always did. The car slowly rolled out of the driveway and started up the street, the engine a perfect purr.

He did love that car, but why shouldn't he? He'd taken a wreck that belonged to his dad and returned it to something beautiful, high-gloss yellow with a thick black stripe up the middle of the hood. He'd done all the work himself. For a guy with a degree in history, he knew more about cars than anybody I knew.

Red brake lights flashed as he came to a full and complete stop at the end of the block. I counted in my head—*one thousand and one, one thousand and two, one thousand and three*—the way my dad had taught me when I was too little to know he was teaching me. The brake lights went off, and he turned the corner and was gone.

I never worried about my dad in his car. Even when he was furious, he drove calmly and in control. There were times I'd practically begged him to "open it up," but he always kept it close to the limits. My dad said you could tell a lot about how somebody lived by the way they drove.

Sometimes he'd take me out and we'd drive for hours, going no place but going there together. He was the driver and I was the DJ. I loved driving with—

I heard my mom coming up the stairs.

I ducked into my room and slid into bed, pulling up the covers, grabbing a pillow and turning toward the wall. I couldn't hear her anymore, so she had either turned around or was deliberately trying to be quiet. I kept pretending to be asleep, not moving, hardly breathing, eyes closed tightly, hiding under the covers in the darkness. There was no way of knowing if she was standing in my doorway without revealing myself. I'd wait. Even if she was there, she'd go away.

"Jordie?" she asked softly.

I worked at not startling. I continued to play at being asleep.

"Jordie," she said a little louder.

She always called me Jordie. My dad always went with my full name, Jordan. He'd named me after his hero, Michael Jordan. My friends usually called me J.R.—Jordan Ryker—but my best friend, Junior, called me Jay. He thought it was cool to shorten names and words, as if communicating in code.

"Jordie, are you asleep?"

Faking sleep wasn't working. When my mom decided on something, she didn't stop until it happened. That was probably why all this fighting was driving her nuts—she hadn't been able to fix things. I rolled over. She stood at the door before coming a few steps closer.

"Were you asleep?"

"I *was* asleep." I sat up and did a fake yawn as I stretched my arms.

"I thought your father and I might have been keeping you awake."

"I don't see him, so I guess it's only *you* keeping me awake."

I instantly felt bad and was glad it was too dark to see her expression.

"Sorry...I didn't mean that. I was awake. Honestly, it wasn't that loud."

She sat down on the edge of my bed. That meant she was going to talk and that I would need to talk or at least listen.

"He left," she said. "Your father took off in that car of his. Again."

When they were fighting, he was *my father*. When they weren't, he was Chris. He'd been called "my father" a lot in the last three weeks.

"I wish he'd stay and talk it through instead of running away," she said.

"He was driving, not running."

"You know what I mean. You remember to never do that with your—"

"Wife," I said, completing the sentence. "How about I get a girlfriend before you marry me off?"

"You could have lots of girlfriends if you wanted," she said. "You're smart and kind and good-looking."

"Spoken like a true mother."

"No! Spoken because it's true. Especially with basketball season coming up. What girl can resist a basketball star? I know I couldn't," she said with a sad sigh.

I knew the story. My parents had met in college. He was on the basketball team, and she watched the games.

"Funny how I didn't even like basketball, but I'll never forget the first time I saw your father in his cute little shorts and—"

"Could we please, *please* not go there?"

"Sorry," she said. "It's just such a wonderful memory. A happy reminder."

I knew the story so well I could have told it myself. In fact, sometimes I'd mouth the words along with my parents to make fun of them. It was so scripted it could have been a movie.

Mom had reluctantly begun going to games in college because her then-boyfriend was a fan. But she'd started to like the action and feel part of the cheering fans as she began to understand the game and know the players. When she and her boyfriend broke up, she kept going to the games with her friends, and she started paying more and more attention to one player. My dad. She decided she wanted to get to know him.

My mom found out where his residence was on campus, where he got coffee and when he went to the gym for practices. She put herself in places where they could "accidentally" bump into each other. So, basically, my mom stalked my dad. When they finally met and started talking, it was my mom who asked my dad out for coffee, then to a movie. It went from casual to serious, and they dated all through the rest of their time at college. She'd been not just a stalker but a very determined and successful stalker. I wouldn't be here if she hadn't been. Of course, right here, right now, with her sitting on the edge of my bed in the dark, there were a few other places I wanted to be.

"He gives more to that car than he does to us," she said.

That was one of the places I would have rather been right now—in that car. I was pretty sure we'd be listening to music if I were, and I was completely sure we wouldn't be talking about them fighting. My dad would have let me play whatever music I wanted.

"Look, I really have to get to sleep," I said. "I do have basketball tryouts tomorrow, remember?"

"Sorry, of course. You know, basketball is pretty important to me too."

She got up, leaned over and gave me a big hug. "I love you, Jordie."

"I love you too, Mom."

She squeezed me even tighter and held on. How long was this going to last? Several seconds later she let me go.

"Do you want me to leave it open?" She hesitated at the door.

"Closed, please."

"There's nothing to worry about," she said.

I knew she wasn't speaking to me, but I answered anyway. "I'm not worried. I'm tired."

She closed the door. The room became darker. And better. Why did she think I would be worried? They fought. It happened. It had been happening for years. They got over it. Tomorrow he'd be downstairs making breakfast, and they'd be acting like it had never happened and everything was all right.

Acting—that word stuck in my head. That's what it felt like. They were both acting. Maybe all of us were acting, but more and more I was losing track of what roles we were supposed to be playing.

I reached out toward my night table and fumbled for my phone. There was somebody I did want to talk to. Hopefully I wouldn't be waking him up, but even if I did, he wouldn't mind.

Two

The phone rang once before I heard "Hey, Jay."

"Hey, Junior. Did I wake you up?"

"No, I was just lying here scrolling through posts."

"Anything interesting?"

"New unis for the Spurs."

"Unis?"

"Uniforms. What did you think I meant? Unicorns?"

"Is uniform too long to say?" I asked.

"Two syllables are better than three. Have I taught you nothing?"

"Basically, no, but that wasn't why I called."

"I figured you called because you're nervous about the tryouts and you're hoping I can work my magic at point guard to make you look less awful."

"You? Help me? Between setting hard screens, continually drawing a double team to give you open shots and cleaning up your misses, I've been carrying *you* for the last seven years!"

"You carrying me! My back hurts just thinking about carrying a load as big as you. Do you know how much work I do?"

"The only thing you're working is your gums."

He chuckled. "My gums? That's the best you can do?"

"It's late. I'm tired."

"Trash talk has always been the worst part of your game," he said.

Junior did know my game. Better than anybody. We met almost seven years ago, as six-year-olds on the same house-league team. We were on the same travel team, in the same school, in the same class some years, and we had been best friends all those years.

"Okay, so why *did* you call?" Junior asked.

I hesitated. Was I really going to tell him I called because my parents were fighting?

"Did your parents get into it again?" he asked.

I laughed. Why had I thought he wouldn't know?

"Yeah, but what else is new."

"Not new, but more often. Don't you think?"

Junior would know. He spent a lot of time at our place. It wasn't unusual for him to have dinner with us at least twice a week. An added bonus was that my parents never openly fought in front of him. It was more subtle or silent.

"But it's over, right?"

"My father went for a drive."

"Oh, then I better get off the phone and get ready," Junior said.

"Ready for what?"

"Ready to be picked up. Didn't you know that when he takes off, he comes over and takes me for a drive? I'm sort of the son he wishes he'd had…smart, tough, good ballplayer, smooth talker."

"You're such a jerk."

"That's the jealousy talking."

He was just joking, of course, but really, he was as close to a second son to my dad and a brother to me as a person could be.

"I really do love that Camaro," he said.

"It's pretty good."

"Pretty good?" he exclaimed, sounding offended. "That car is much more than pretty good. It's your second-best chance."

"I'm almost afraid to ask. My second-best chance for what?"

"Of ever, and I mean, *ever*, getting a girlfriend."

"And my best chance?" I asked.

"Me, of course. We have to hope that someday you'll learn from me."

I wasn't even going to argue this. He was as comfortable with girls as I was uncomfortable. He was smoother with them than he was with a basketball, and that was saying a lot, because Junior was a baller. He said it was because he was raised by a single mom, but really it was because Junior was fearless with them.

"Of course, if you could read women the way you read a defense, you'd have no problems," Junior said.

"Women?"

"Don't get technical with me. Girls become women long before boys become men."

"Now you're sounding like my mother," I said.

"Who do you think I learned that from?" he asked. "Seriously, are you okay?"

"Sure, I'm fine."

"You know you can come over here to get away from it. Anytime."

"I know." Not that I would. "I just wanted to say hello."

"That's never a prob."

"Problem is too long to say? I'm hanging up. Good night."

"Sure. Night. Talk to you in the a.m."

He hung up, and I put down the phone. I really did need to get to sleep, and now maybe I could.

The house smelled of cinnamon and yeast. My dad was back home. I knew it before I was even really awake.

Since the announcement that the plant would be closing, my mom worked earlier or later whenever she could, and my dad had taken on more of the house stuff. Shortly after the announcement, he'd taken up baking. It turned out he was really good at it.

He began with muffins. He started with classic sweet ones, then moved on to things like provolone and prosciutto with fig. He made some killer muffins. After that he became obsessed with bread. He even brought home an old scale from the plant to weigh everything out, and he made his own sourdough by letting the bacteria in the air get into some flour and water left out for a few days. He kept and fed the mother yeast in some old glazed earthenware jars Mom found for him at a garage sale. It seemed weird to me to feed bread, but it was what he did.

Dad was hunched over the counter, his body rocking as he kneaded the dough, when I came down the stairs.

"Good night's sleep?" he asked as I pulled out a stool on the opposite side of the counter from him. "Careful, those muffins are still hot."

I took one and peeled off the paper. The steam escaped from it and disappeared.

"Not bad," I answered, pretending the previous night hadn't happened.

"I added some cardamom and ginger. Let me know what you think."

He was pretending too. We sat in silence, him stopping his kneading every so often to check the time and take sips of his coffee. Bread had to be kneaded only so long, and Dad was precise. Sweat beaded on his temples. He wiped it away on the back of his forearms.

"They're good," I said.

"Better with the extra spices?" he asked.

"I think you could use even more."

He opened the oven door, pulled out a plate piled high with pancakes and put it down on the table.

"Blueberry, lemon–poppy seed and pumpkin."

"Pumpkin?"

"Don't knock it until you try it. Besides, you usually put on so much maple syrup that I could feed you cardboard and you'd ask for seconds."

He went to the fridge, pulled out the syrup and set it on the table.

I examined the pancakes. It was easy to identify which was which. I took two pumpkin to start and poured on the syrup.

"This is really good," I said.

"Don't sound so surprised."

Dad finished with his dough, shaped it into a big ball and placed a bowl over it so it could rest and rise. He poured some milk and slid it across the counter to me. I liked being alone with him like this, where we didn't need to say too much.

Mom came into the kitchen, and I held my breath, waiting.

"Good morning, honey," Dad sang out.

"You too." She came over, stood on tiptoe and gave him a kiss on the cheek.

I let out my breath. Everything was normal—or, at least, appeared to be normal.

My mom's hair was still wet from the shower. She was dressed for the office. She worked at the big-box store one town over.

"You've been busy," she said as she got herself a cup of coffee.

Dad opened the fridge and pulled out the cream. He poured it into her mug.

"Jordan needs to load up on some carbs before the big tryouts. I'd rather he put something half-decent in him."

Mom picked up a muffin. "With all the wonderful baking you're doing, I should be careful."

Dad looked my mom over. "You've never had an issue looking good, Mandy."

Mom stood a bit taller as she sipped her coffee. I saw her smile into her cup.

It was all gross to me, but my parents flirting a little was better than them fighting a lot. In fact, when they weren't fighting, they usually got along so well that I wondered— were they acting when they weren't fighting or when they were? What I knew this morning was that it had all blown over. They actually seemed to be good with one another.

Mom finished her coffee. "I should get going. I'll take the truck and fill it up."

I was sure she said that to make peace.

"I have to get going too," my dad said. "There's a meeting at the plant."

"But isn't this your day off?" she asked.

"There have been some issues with quality control."

"More than normal?"

"Up by almost 200 percent."

"With the plant closing, I guess you can't blame people."

"That's no excuse," my dad stated. "We're dealing with people's lives. People's families. People pay good money for their cars and rely on us to produce safe, quality ones." He turned to me. "If you're playing a game and you're down by twenty points with two minutes left, how do you play?"

"The best you can. The same as you always do," I answered.

"I guess I get a little worked up and emotional about this stuff," my dad said.

"It's one of the things I love about you, how much you care," my mom said.

My dad cleared my plate. "The meeting is at seven thirty, so unless you want to walk, Jordan, I'll have to drop you off at school early."

"Can we still pick up Junior?"

"Doesn't that go without saying? I half expect him to be sitting in the car when we get out there."

"I'll let him know."

I got up and grabbed a couple more muffins to put in my backpack, one for me, one for Junior.

Three

"I can't believe you don't hear it," my dad said.

"It sounds fine." I didn't hear anything wrong.

My dad revved the engine.

Junior leaned forward from the back seat. "I can definitely hear it. It sort of flutters."

"Exactly! There's something off in the carb's air-to-fuel ratio. I'll adjust it tonight."

He pulled away from the stop sign, and I felt myself being pushed slightly back into the seat as he accelerated.

"Keep pushin' it, Mr. R!" Junior yelled.

My dad shifted into second. The car jumped in response. He pushed it harder and harder and then shut it back down to regular speed.

"Don't you ever want to open it up all the way?" Junior asked.

"Too much power. Not enough road."

"Come on, Mr. R. If anybody can handle this car, you can!"

Junior reached over the seat. The two of them exchanged

a high five. My dad liked Junior a lot. I thought Junior liked my father even more. Junior had never really gotten to know his dad. My dad more than made up for that.

An oncoming car approached. The driver waved. My dad waved back. That happened all the time. Dad had lived here his whole life. He knew people and people knew him—and his car. And because so many people knew him, they also knew me. I heard "Hey, you're Chris's boy, aren't you?" a lot.

"What do you know about your new coach?" my dad asked.

He was asking about Mr. Tanner, who had just transferred to the school, taught math and had agreed to coach the team.

"He's a good enough guy," I said.

"I know lots of good guys. Does he know basketball?" Dad asked.

"We've talked basketball with him," I answered.

"Yeah, he knows stuff," Junior chirped from the back seat. "Not like you, of course. But for a school coach."

Mr. Tanner was a basketball fan, but he'd never coached a team before. Junior and I were keeping that on the down-low from my father. We knew he'd make a big deal about it. School ball was different than travel ball. Most of the school coaches were nice people who knew a little bit of the sport. You couldn't expect any of them to know basketball the way my father knew the game.

We pulled up to the school. There was nobody in the yard, only a couple of cars in the parking lot. Neither of them belonged to Mr. Tanner.

"Sorry about getting you here so early. This meeting is important."

"Is it about the closing?" Junior asked.

"Everything is about the closing."

"Thanks for driving us, Mr. R. You're the best," Junior said. "Being early is no problem. We've got a ball. We can fool around on the outdoor hoop until somebody lets us in the building."

We climbed out. Before I closed the door, my father leaned over so he could see us. "Remember, practice the way you play."

"Yes, sir," Junior said. I nodded.

My father winked at me, tapped two fingers on his chest above his heart and pointed at me—his silent way of saying "I love you." I did the same before I closed the door, making sure not to slam it. He drove away while we stood and watched.

"Your dad is way cooler than you are. You know that, right?"

I was going to argue, but there wasn't any point in encouraging him. Besides, he really did like my dad.

"That car looks fast even when it's driving slow," Junior remarked.

"It looks fast when it's sitting in the garage. It sucks that my dad is too afraid to open it up."

"When *you* own it, you can drive it fast."

We walked into the schoolyard. We passed the side doors, the ones that led into the gym. I pulled at one to make sure they were locked. They were. Junior bounced the ball as we walked, putting it back and forth through his legs, crossing over, eyes up, taking a few side moves to get around imagined defenders. He *was* good.

Junior flashed me a pass as we hit the court. I put up a shot. It bounced off the rim and shot on a diagonal across the yard. I raced after the ball, retrieved it and threw up a second that fell short of the net completely.

A ball sailed past from somewhere behind me and swooshed through the hoop.

"Three points. Nothing. But. Net."

I turned. There was Aaron, looking smug. He was new to the school this year. He could play some ball—he played forward too—but he wasn't as good as he thought he was. He'd definitely make the team, but unless I really messed up, starting power forward was all mine.

His sister, Tammy, darted past me and retrieved both balls. While running, she shot each one in rapid succession. Both balls hit the backboard and sank into the net.

"Two, four. I'm in the lead," she called. She was a year younger than us but was in our grade. She'd skipped fifth grade completely because she was gifted. Her backpack was covered with buttons from all sorts of organizations, and she talked about how backward our school was compared to where they'd come from.

Tammy had made a case to the principal that girls should be allowed to join the boys' tryouts. That was why she was here with us. As far as I was concerned, if she was good enough to make the team, she deserved to be here.

"Air, Tam! 'Sup?" Junior asked.

"If I'm Tam, then maybe we should call you June," Tammy teased.

Junior grinned at her. "You can call me June if you want, as long as you're calling." He gave her a wink that took nearly half his face to execute.

Tammy laughed. She scooped up one of the balls and passed it to him.

"How about a little competition?" she asked. "Me and my brother against the two of you."

"You definitely got that right," Junior said. "Us playing against you will be very little competition. But we'll take it easy on you."

"Not if Jordan keeps missing those easy ones," Aaron said under his breath as he pushed past me, bumping my shoulder with his.

Junior did some fancy dribbling and started to spin, almost twirling around Tammy, who laughed as she swiped to get the ball away. But her timing was off. Aaron shook his head and ran at Junior, who passed the ball behind his back to me.

I caught the pass and had the ball only a second before I launched it from the top of the key and got a three-pointer.

"Seriously, Tammy!" Aaron barked.

Aaron scowled as Tammy laughed. She pulled her hair back and used a hair band that had been on her wrist to fasten a ponytail.

"Nice shot, but it was also a nice pass. I need to take you more seriously, June," she said, laughing. "Otherwise my brother is going to lose it on me."

It had been our basket, so it was our ball in—basic two-on-two rules.

Junior took the ball and started showing off. He tried some moves around Tammy, almost doing a breakdance. She swatted the ball away. Still smiling, Tammy faked a pass to Aaron, and in the few seconds it took Junior to figure out she still had the ball, she threw up a shot, and the ball dropped. It was obvious she had some game.

The doors to the gym opened. Mr. Tanner popped his head out. He waved to us. It was time to move things inside.

We were the first four in the gym. Mr. Tanner was in shorts and T-shirt, whistle around his neck and clipboard in his hands. We were getting ready to restart our game at the far hoop when he called for Junior and me to come over.

"Morning, guys," he said. "I was wondering if we could talk for a second."

Junior nodded. "Of course, Coach."

"Sure," I said.

His iPad was only partially hidden by the clipboard. I could see the article on the screen, which was titled "Twelve Basketball Drills to Evaluate Players." Thank goodness my father wasn't here to see this.

"You two have been playing ball for years, right?"

"Forever."

"Good. I've been reading up and everything, but I was hoping you two could assist."

"We can help for sure, Coach," I said.

"And Aaron could help too," Junior added.

I shot him a dirty look.

"He's played travel ball. He knows his stuff." Junior looked at me. "He does."

"That would be great. Thanks, guys."

Even with our help, things didn't go smoothly. There were too many students trying out and too many that didn't know basketball. Things got a little out of hand. Players arrived hungry for spots on the team but no appetite for the game.

Besides me, only Junior and Aaron—as much as I didn't really like him—had guaranteed spots. The rest were what my father would call—from the Clint Eastwood western—the good, the bad and the ugly. I'd never seen the movie but knew what he meant. And really, on a school team, all it took was three great players to do really, really well.

I looked across the gym. Tammy fumbled a pass, recovered and tried for a basket she was never going to make. The ball bounced off the side of the backboard and out-of-bounds. She panted as she pushed her hair back off her sweaty forehead.

Junior trotted over to her. He started talking and motioning like he was throwing and then receiving a pass—he had been open if she'd gotten the ball to him. Tammy nodded.

The coach blew his whistle and yelled, "Water break, two minutes!"

Junior came over to me by the benches. "She's not bad."

"She's got more potential than half the guys here," I said. I took a swig of water.

"She should have stuck to playing with the girls," Aaron said. Obviously he'd overheard us. He drank some water too. "I told her she wasn't going to make the cut."

"How'd that go over?" asked Junior.

Aaron smirked. "How do you think? She told me she was winning by finishing the tryouts, and it didn't matter if she made the team. This is basketball, not some protest march. She should go hold up a sign and bang a drum. Boys play with boys, and girls play with girls. It's as simple as that."

"Wow, Air," Junior said. "That's messed. Women rock basketball."

"I think she's got a shot at making the team," I said.

"What?" Aaron asked.

"She's not bad."

"I'm not saying she's bad. I showed her everything she knows."

"Including that last shot where she bounced it off the side of the backboard?" I joked.

"You got something more you want to say?" he asked.

"Lots. Women play basketball all over the world. They have their own leagues. They compete in the Olympics," I said. I took another swig from my bottle.

Aaron rolled his eyes. "There's a word for that type of woman."

Junior choked on his water, but before either of us could respond, Coach blew his whistle and yelled for us all to bring it in.

We gathered around him, some of us taking a knee at the front.

"You all worked hard out there. You should feel proud of your efforts, gentlemen."

Tammy cleared her throat.

"And ladies, pardon me," Coach said with a nod to Tammy. "We have two more tryouts to determine who's going to make this year's team," he continued. "Hit the showers, and get yourselves ready for class."

Junior clapped me on the shoulder as we headed off the court.

"Nice job," I said.

"You too. But we already know we've got spots."

"Not that. With Tammy. Showing her that you were open for a pass. Smooth," I said.

Junior pulled his hand from my shoulder. "It wasn't like that."

"Sure. Sure."

"You jealous or something?" Junior asked.

"What's there to be jealous of?" I shot back, thinking about the way Junior had so easily run up to Tammy and showed her what to do.

Junior did that exaggerated wink that took the entire side of his face. "Sure. Sure."

"What does that mean?" I asked.

"Nothing at all." Junior did the dumb wink again before erupting into a laughing fit.

Four

At noon we returned to the gym, which doubled as our school's cafeteria. Lunchtime supervisors, mostly mothers of kids in the school, walked between tables. They could be heard telling kids to find a seat, make sure to clean up their mess or to hurry up and eat. We used to have a problem finding enough supervisors to do the job, but lately, with the upcoming plant closure, there were more people who wanted the work.

I claimed an empty table on the center circle. This was my usual spot, and I was always quick to grab it. Junior took the seat opposite me and pulled out a plastic bag tied at the top. Junior always had way too much food for himself. His mom cooked as if catering a party. There were usually a lot of leftovers at his place.

"My father made muffins," I told Junior.

"Trade? I've got some pancit, some lumpia and some suman. My mom had a burst of energy between her shifts at the ER."

I slid a muffin across the table. Anything Junior's mom made was really good. My family had really come to appreciate Filipino cuisine thanks to her. She cooked in big batches and always made sure to send some over to our place. She made my favorite, adobo, regularly because she knew how much I liked it. After Junior's dad had died, and with his mom's relatives all overseas, our families had kind of adopted each other.

"What did you think of tryouts?" Junior asked.

I shrugged.

"And Coach?" Junior dished up some of everything onto the lid of a container and pushed it across the table to me. I dug in immediately.

"He's going to need a lot of work," I said around the pancit I was stuffing into my mouth. Boy, Junior's mom really knew how to cook.

"If your dad had been there, he'd have had a hard time sitting in the bleachers watching how Mr. Tanner coached," Junior remarked as he chewed the muffin.

Aaron plunked down in a seat beside Junior. He didn't usually sit with us, and I almost told him the seat was taken, but that would have been more unfriendly than I wanted to be.

"What's that?" Aaron asked.

"My lunch," Junior replied.

"Yeah, I figured, but whatever it is, it smells bad," Aaron said. "Don't you eat sandwiches wherever you're from?"

"He's *from* Franklin. He was born here," I said. "Same as his dad and his dad's dad and his dad's dad's dad and..."

"Then what's with the weird food?"

"I'm half Filipino. These are my foods," Junior explained more patiently than I thought Aaron deserved.

Tammy appeared at the table. "Can I join you?"

"Anytime," Junior said. He pushed out a chair for her.

I almost said, Thanks for asking, but I only thought it. She had more manners than her brother.

"Wow. That looks so good," Tammy said. "So much more interesting than my boring cheese sandwich."

Aaron rolled his eyes at his sister. "Don't you have somewhere else to sit?"

"Nope," Tammy said.

"There are some girls your age a few tables over." Aaron pointed. "It's bad enough you got bumped into my grade and insisted on trying out for basketball. You don't need to be part of my entire life."

Tammy ignored him. "What kind of spring rolls are those?"

"They're called lumpia," Junior told her. He held one out to her. "This one's ground pork and vegetables."

"Yum. I miss all the different types of food we could get in the city," Tammy said as she took the roll from Junior. "You could eat food from a different country every night if you wanted."

"I never wanted," Aaron said. He took a big bite of his sandwich. "No one seems to care what I want though."

"I'm going to speak to the principal," Tammy continued, "and see if we can do some more interesting menus on Fridays instead of the same old pizza lunches."

"I love za Fridays!" Junior exclaimed. "Not my za!"

"Can't you just say the whole word *pizza*?" I asked.

"Less syllables is better syllables," he replied.

"I'm surprised you don't call them 'sylls.'"

"Regardless, wouldn't you like to try new things?" Tammy asked Junior.

"There she goes again," Aaron mumbled loudly.

"These are delicious," Tammy said, holding up her remaining piece of lumpia. "Shouldn't the whole school get to try these? Back home, the Social Justice Club brought all sorts of different cuisines to our cafeteria. We were offering plant-based diet options before any other school in the city. Franklin's going to need a lot of work if it ever wants to catch up."

I bit into an apple and didn't say a word. I didn't think it was fair that Tammy was insulting our whole town when her family had barely begun to live here. She didn't even know anything about Franklin, and she'd already decided we needed to be fixed.

"As I remember, no one at our old school bought that meat alternative because it smelled worse than Junior's lunch," Aaron replied.

"Junior's lunch smells wonderful! And tastes even better," she said as she popped her last piece of lumpia in her mouth. Junior offered another, and Tammy took it.

"Look, you offered food no one would buy, and that was in the city. It definitely won't fly here, where their gym is their cafeteria!"

"That's why we need action," Tammy said and pointed

her already half-eaten lumpia at her brother. "Things won't change if everyone's happy with the status quo."

"You don't even hear yourself, do you?" Aaron asked. "No one understands what you're saying. That's probably why the principal didn't fight you when you wanted to try out for the boys' basketball team. She didn't know what you were talking about. Boys. Not girls. It says so right in the name."

"Gender is a construct," Tammy said, taking another bite of lumpia.

"Why shouldn't Tam try out? If she's a strong player, why wouldn't our team want her on it?" Junior asked.

"And women began playing basketball almost as soon as the sport was invented. I read all about it," I said.

"Then let her try out for the girls' team."

"And Pat Summitt has the most wins in college-level coaching of all time. And a lot of the rules of men's basketball were being used by women for decades before we implemented them," I said.

I didn't just love playing basketball. I studied its history in my spare time.

Tammy smiled at me. It was a big, friendly smile that even reached her eyes. I looked down at the table, feeling myself go warm and red.

"What's wrong with all of you? It's a boys' team!" Aaron exclaimed.

A passing lunchtime supervisor shushed Aaron.

"This is messed up," Aaron declared, shoving the remainder of his lunch back into his bag. "Girls' bodies are different than ours. They can't physically compete with us. The rest of the girls know it. That's why they didn't try out. Maybe that's why they aren't your friends."

That was a low blow, I thought.

"Look who's talking. You aren't exactly Mr. Popularity. Maybe other girls didn't try out because they never thought they could," Tammy said.

"Maybe you think too much. You want to play, then before the next tryouts you should grow a set to be like one of the guys."

"Maybe you should grow a brain."

"Maybe you should grow some boobs and do something worthwhile, like starting a cheerleading squad!" Aaron snapped.

"Come on, dude," Junior interjected. "Too far."

"She's your sister," I added.

"You think I don't know that?" Aaron abruptly stood up. "Whatever. I've got to get to detention anyway. See you on the court, where the best *man* wins." Aaron threw his bag over one shoulder, left our table and shoved both gymnasium doors open as he exited.

"You okay?" Junior asked Tammy.

"I'm fine," Tammy replied. Her words didn't match the quiver in her voice. She wasn't as tough as she liked to act.

Junior shrugged. "What he said was garbage. I hate that stuff. And 'sides, he's wrong."

"Of course he is," Tammy said.

Junior offered Tammy his last lumpia. "I hope if he makes the team, he handles a ball better than he handles his mouth."

I nodded stupidly in agreement.

Tammy let out a big sigh, and her shoulders seemed to relax.

"Our mom says big mouths run in our family. At least he comes by it honestly. Thanks for having my back."

"Anytime," Junior said.

I looked up from my muffin to see Tammy smiling at me. Junior was smiling at both of us.

I shoved a big piece of muffin into my mouth and gave a double thumbs-up.

"So let's talk tryouts," Junior said, leaning across the table toward Tammy. "You've got the team's two star players at your disposal. We could walk you through some of the drills that will be coming."

"Really?" she asked.

"Why not?" I asked. "We really do like *one* member of your family."

Junior laughed. "Smooth, man, very smooth."

Five

We hit the court outside after school. Junior did all the talking, setting us up. Tammy clenched her jaw and dove into the drills. She didn't talk much, mainly listened and nodded. That suited me fine because I didn't exactly know what to say. I knew basketball, but I really didn't know girls. Junior was fluent in both. Whenever Junior offered a suggestion, Tammy picked it up. She learned fast.

After about an hour, Tammy said she had to get home.

Junior and I gave each other a look to confirm we'd head back to my place for dinner. Junior's mother was at the hospital still, and he could chill a few hours before my dad drove him home. We took turns dribbling the ball, making passes back and forth as we walked.

"So what do you think of Tammy?" Junior asked.

"She can play some ball."

"I wasn't talking about basketball," he said. "What do you think of *her*?"

"What's to think?"

"For a smart guy, you can be thick. She's pretty."

I shrugged.

"And she likes you."

"Me?" I asked.

"I find it hard to believe too, especially when she has the choice of you or me. But she does."

"If she likes me so much, why does she spend all her time talking to you?" I asked.

"I'm the way to get to you."

Junior threw me a hard pass. It bounced off my fingers and into the road. I took a quick look—no traffic—and retrieved the ball.

"I think she has potential," Junior said as I rejoined him.

"Potential for what?"

"B-ball, of course. Try to get your head out of the gutter."

Coming up to my house, I could see both of my parents had beaten us home. The truck was parked on the street in front of our house. The Camaro was almost at the end of the driveway, leaving clear the regulation basketball key Dad had painted on the pavement.

"You want to play?" Junior asked.

"What a dumb question. But how about we eat first?"

Junior bounced the basketball he was carrying with two hands before he lobbed it over to me. I took a hook shot and scored, the ball bouncing and rolling onto the grass.

The house smelled like oregano, basil, garlic and olive oil. Which meant my dad had turned the dough from that morning into focaccia. It rarely lasted long enough to see a second day.

"Hey, Mr. and Mrs. R. Smells great. What's cooking?" Junior called.

Mom was still in her suit, her hair a mess of curls that cradled the light they caught. She gave Junior a smile that seemed a bit too big.

"I brought home some Tuscan white bean soup from work. It was on sale, and your dad seems to know how to doctor it," Mom said.

"And your focaccia, right, Mr. R?" Junior said.

"You got it, Junior," my dad replied. He seemed a bit off too. "Dinner's not ready yet."

"Jay, can you lend me something to change into?" Junior asked. "I think we both stink!"

"Speak for yourself!"

"To tell the truth," my dad said, "you both should wash up and change into something else."

"Maybe I can borrow a belt, Mrs. R. One of Jay's shirts might as well be a dress on me."

It was true. I'd had a growth spurt recently and shot up. Junior wasn't tall, and if he took after his mom, he never would be. His height was often an advantage on the court. The closer to the floor, the better the handle on the dribble.

I showered while Junior got some homework done, and then we switched. Afterward we headed downstairs, making plans for a game of Horse after dinner. Maybe my parents would even join in. They seemed the most comfortable together when they were on the court.

Mom ladled out bowls of soup while Dad sliced the bread and put it on the table.

Junior and I chose seats closest to the bread and grabbed the biggest pieces we saw. Junior ripped off a hunk, shoved it in his mouth, then ripped off another and dropped it in his soup bowl.

My mom put a napkin beside Junior's bowl and put another piece of bread on it.

Dad was the last to sit.

"Pass the pepper, please," Mom said to my dad.

He wrinkled his nose but didn't move to give her the pepper. "You didn't even try it. I added pepper. I even added pepper flakes."

"We've had this soup before. I like lots of pepper."

"Why do you keep buying it when it's not really a good product to start with?" Dad asked.

"It's economical," Mom said, "especially considering the amount we get for the price. With my employee discount, it doesn't make sense not to buy it."

"Except it's full of sodium."

"Then add more water."

"And wash out the flavor you have me fix?"

"It wouldn't be a big deal if you handed me the pepper," she said.

"You didn't even try it yet."

My mom crumpled up her napkin. She looked like

she had something to say as she stood up. Instead she just walked to the fridge. She pulled out some hot sauce and began shaking it into her soup bowl.

"Can I get a little of that?" Junior asked, holding his bowl toward my mom with both hands. He was already almost finished.

Mom put the bottle down near Junior, who shook way too much into his soup and then shoved a huge spoonful into his mouth. He began guzzling down water as soon as he swallowed. His eyes grew wider the more he gulped down.

"Eat some bread," my mom instructed as she handed Junior another piece.

My dad shook his head at her. She caught it out of the corner of her eye.

"How'd the meeting go?" Junior asked my dad once his mouth wasn't on fire anymore.

"Not bad. Cooler heads prevailed, and we got some issues sorted out."

My mom scoffed.

"Something wrong?" he asked.

"When I asked you about the meeting, you said there was nothing to talk about."

"There wasn't."

"But now you're talking about it." My mom's tone sounded a lot like my dad's—cool, calm, in control.

"I don't want to fight about this," he said.

"Nobody is fighting. I'd like to be part of the discussion. So how did the meeting go?"

"We have a guest, Mandy."

"I'm here way too much to still be a guest. I'm almost like furniture now. Furniture that eats really spicy food. Man, that was hot."

"You're not furniture," I said, looking from Junior to my parents. "He's not furniture. Do you two get that?"

"Jordan—" my dad began.

"Look, I should go," Junior said as he nearly popped out of his seat. He plastered on my mom's too-big-to-be-real smile as he cleared his bowl to the counter.

"You don't have to go," Dad said.

"Yes, please stay," my mom added.

"No. You should go. It would be good for you to go," I said.

My parents and Junior looked surprised.

Junior nodded. "I've got some homework to do. Maybe we can play that game of Horse another time."

"Sure. Another time," I said.

"Let me give you a ride," my dad offered.

Junior fumbled as he pulled on his sneakers. "I'm good. Really. I'll be home by the time you grab your keys. Later, Mr. and Mrs. R. See you tomorrow, Jay."

"See you."

Once Junior had left, I stood to clear my dishes. I hadn't touched any of the soup.

"Jordie?" Mom asked.

I didn't reply and started to walk out of the kitchen.

"Answer your mother, Jordan."

I nearly snorted. "You're kidding, right?" I kept walking out of the room.

"Don't walk away, young man," my dad warned.

"Seriously?" I turned around in the doorway. "You're telling *me* not to walk away? Would it be better if I drove away?"

Mom snorted. That wasn't what I'd intended. This wasn't about him—it was about both of them.

"And maybe when you and Dad decide to start something, Junior doesn't have to be here. It's bad enough you can't stop fighting when I'm around, but don't have one of your 'little disagreements' in front of my best friend. You two don't even get how to fight. No one fights about stupid soup."

I ran up to my room and slammed the door.

I heard the rumble of my parents, who began arguing in earnest now that I was upstairs.

I grabbed my basketball and began bouncing it hard against the floor. Over and over. I wasn't allowed to bounce the ball in the house. The hollow reverberations of the ball hitting the floor sent tinny echoes throughout my room, drowning out my parents with every dribble. I knew they couldn't avoid hearing it.

With every bounce I wished I had left with Junior. I wished I had gone to his house and left my parents to argue over whatever spice was in whatever dish they decided was worth fighting over. I held the ball and threw it, one-handed, as hard as I could at my bedroom door. The sound was like a cannon being fired.

I caught the ball, held it and listened. The fighting had stopped.

I walked to the front window as quietly as I could, expecting to see my dad's taillights flashing red at the stop sign at the end of the block. The Camaro was still in the driveway. I imagined being in the passenger seat, driving away. Except my dad wasn't driving. No one was. Sometimes that's how it felt. I was being driven, but nobody was at the wheel.

Now, even with the fighting having stopped, and even though my dad hadn't driven off, it felt like the house was holding its breath, waiting for something to happen.

Six

I lay on my back, throwing my basketball in the air and catching it as it dropped into my open hands. Over and over.

I assumed it was my mom when I heard the knock on the door. I figured the little disagreement had finally flamed out and my dad had finally driven off into the night. Maybe my mom wanted to have another of our little chats where she did nothing to relieve either of our worries.

The door opened. It was my father. "C'mon. I'm going for a ride and want you to come along—if you want to."

"Of course." I nearly tripped getting my shoes on as I headed down the stairs.

Mom was standing beside the door. "See you later," she said to both of us as she closed it behind us.

We climbed into the car, and my dad readjusted the mirrors. He craned his neck as he backed out of the driveway and pulled into the road. The engine purred, but this time I could hear something else. Maybe it was whatever my dad and Junior had heard. He stopped at the stop sign, and I counted from one thousand and one to one thousand and three before my dad proceeded.

I could have turned on the radio, but I didn't. We drove in silence, the only sound coming from the Camaro as it begged my dad to let it loose, to let it do what it was designed to do, to hug the road under it as it flashed through Franklin.

At the town limits my dad kept driving. Was he driving faster than he usually did? I leaned over to look at the speedometer. It wasn't my imagination. He was almost fifteen miles over the limit. Dad noticed me looking. I expected him to slow down, but he didn't.

"You know, my old man used to drive this car way too fast all the time. Back then there was no such thing as photo radar or red-light cameras. It was only a cop pulling you over. That meant my father would never get a ticket in Franklin."

"Why's that?"

"Being the president of the union in a town where everybody had somebody working in the plant meant he was the most important person around."

"Really?"

"I was with him a couple of times when he got pulled over. The cops would just give him a warning, shake his hand and send him on his way, even if he was doing something worse than speeding."

"You mean like being drunk?"

My dad let out a big sigh. "I didn't know you knew about that."

"Mom told me."

"She shouldn't have done that," he snapped.

Oh great, I'd started another fight and—

"But it's probably my fault she did." His voice had softened. "It's natural for her to need to share things. I guess I haven't been the best person to share with. His drinking was one of the reasons we never let him drive you places."

"I didn't know that."

"Of course, back then people often used to drink and drive. Somehow it was acceptable, even something to admire."

I thought about it. I couldn't imagine admiring someone for doing that.

He laughed, but it sounded hollow, like the basketball against the floor of my room. "'A *real* man can handle his booze,' he used to say. My father prided himself on being a real man."

We passed into the next town. Dad slowed down and said, "I decided to fix this car after your grandfather died."

I knew the story. How the car had been left for years in his father's garage. The engine had seized, the body was rusting away, but the frame was good—it had potential. My dad had taken it apart piece by piece and put the whole thing back together by hand.

"You had just turned six when he died. How much do you remember about him?"

"He was big. Almost as big as you."

"I was taller, but he was bigger, in more ways than just outweighing me. What else?"

"I thought he must have had really bad breath," I said.

"Why did you think that?"

"He was always chewing on a mint. There was always one in his mouth or he'd be pulling them out of his pocket. He used to give them to me. They tasted good, but sometimes they had lint on them."

"Those mints weren't because of bad breath. They covered up the smell of the alcohol. I can't stand mint." He paused. "I guess with what you already know, it's okay to tell you this. Your grandfather and I had what you might call a complicated relationship. We never figured out the communication thing. We didn't know how to tell each other the stuff we needed to. We just stopped talking. I didn't even know he'd kept this car until I found it hidden away. There was a lot we should have said. A lot I never said."

I picked at the knee of my jeans.

"Did you know your grandfather thought it was a waste of time for me to go to college?"

I stopped picking. "He did?"

"If it weren't for my playing basketball, and the scholarship, he would have thought it was a complete waste of time. He said that thanks to people like him, you could earn more on the line than you could with some degree."

"I want to go to college."

"You have no choice. Before I'd let you go on the line and build cars, I'd run you over with one!" He paused. "But I guess you working the line at the plant isn't really an option."

Those words sank in. We drove in silence for a while.

"Your grandfather told me that he was so happy when I started working at the plant full-time and so disappointed when I went into management."

"Why?"

"He called me a union traitor. There were times during contract negotiations when he sat on one side of the table, and I sat with the people on the other. Like I said, we had a complicated relationship." He paused. "I guess all of my relationships end up complicated. Sometimes I can't ignore that in the middle of every messed-up relationship I have, there's me and how I choose to do things, right or wrong. I've made mistakes with your mom, and I'm worried I'm going to make them with you too."

"If this is about earlier, it's all right," I said. "But if you and Mom could not fight in front of Junior—"

"Your mom and I need to find a way to stop fighting, period. We've been making a mess of everything, Jordan."

My dad pulled over and turned off the car in front of a closed library.

"Things got away from us. Maybe we never had them to begin with."

I didn't follow what he was saying. I stared out the window at a wire trash bin with a metal *No Littering* sign on it.

"We're not happy. We keep going around and around together, and nothing changes and nothing works. Things keep getting worse. And I don't like who I am anymore. And your mom doesn't like who she is. Something has to change. Something has to give."

"Mom could cut you some slack."

My dad gripped the wheel hard with both hands, at ten and two, and shook his head. "She's trying, Jordan. Don't ever blame her when I'm the one who screws things up. There's stuff I don't know how to say to her, to anyone. Stuff I thought I'd put away." My dad began to laugh that bouncing-basketball laugh again. "For starters, I wasn't supposed to argue with my wife every day and make my son miserable."

"I'm not miserable, Dad."

"I was supposed to be a better parent than my father was."

"You're a great parent!" I exclaimed.

"Not lately. All I've done is screw up—differently than my old man did, but still screwing up. I'm on the verge of losing everything. My job. My wife. Myself. I'm not sure what to do anymore." He hit the steering wheel, and it honked. I jumped slightly in my seat.

I turned to look directly at him. "You're my dad. It doesn't matter how you think you've screwed up—you haven't. At least, not with me. I'm your son. Everybody knows you're a great father."

"You don't know everything, Jordan. Nobody does."

"I know if you're down by twenty points in the last two minutes, you still play your best, same as you always do. A smart guy taught me that." I tapped two fingers on my chest so he'd know where I was coming from.

My dad sat a bit taller in his seat. "I'm worried I've been playing the same as I always do but not playing my best. Your mom and I started talking tonight. Actually talking. We need to talk some more, and we're going to get help doing that. We all need to make some changes so that we can play our best going forward."

I nodded and figured the next time my mom asked for pepper, Dad would pass it to her, and when Dad got a new job, there'd be less fighting.

My dad turned the key in the ignition, adjusted his mirrors, then checked his blind spots before he pulled away from the curb. He turned his signal on and did a three-point turn.

I clicked on the radio and played with the dial, going from static voices to some old song.

"Leave it," Dad said. "I had my first kiss in this car to that song."

"Too much info, Dad."

He laughed. "If your grandfather had known, he'd have been furious."

"I thought he liked Mom."

Under the bluish lights of the streetlamps, I saw a tinge of red flood my dad's cheeks. "It wasn't your mom. It was before her."

"An old girlfriend," I said. It made sense my dad would have had a girlfriend before her.

"Not exactly."

"Dad! You were a dog!"

My dad chortled. "No. Not at all."

We came to a stop sign. I counted to one thousand and five before he focused and pulled forward. The song ended.

"I remember the rush of it. The excitement. The thrill of something new and unknown. I think I need to feel that way again right now. I think that's how I can start to fix things."

We drove home with me playing DJ. The music filled the car, and we didn't need to talk for the rest of the ride home.

We pulled into the driveway. My father turned off the engine and the music stopped. The sudden silence seemed heavy and dangerous and wrong.

I went to climb out, but my father stopped me.

"Hold on a second, Jordan. Before we go inside, you should know your mom and I are really going to talk. There are going to be changes. We're going to make things better. For you and for us."

"Good. I'd like that."

"I hope you'll like it," he said. "I hope you'll like it."

Seven

Coach Tanner blew his whistle, signaling the end of the tryout.

"Everybody get a drink, then join me on the bleachers."

This was the end of the last of the five tryouts. He had originally scheduled three, but we—Junior, Aaron and I—had convinced him to hold two additional sessions. After the first three, he'd cut seventeen players, bringing the total down to eighteen who had taken part in the last two tryouts. Now the job was to cut six and keep twelve.

Junior came up beside me. "He's getting better," he said quietly so nobody else could hear. "He's sounding more like a real coach."

"A coach who can run a tryout. Games are different. You know that."

"We helped him learn how to run a tryout. We can help him learn how to coach a game," Junior said. "He's got potential."

We took long slugs from our water bottles and joined

the people sitting in the section of bleachers near Coach, who was looking down at his clipboard.

"Okay, let's get started," he called out. "I want to thank all of you for coming to the tryouts. We have enough talent to have a great team. Maybe the problem is we have too much talent. I feel bad having to cut anybody in this gym."

"Then keep us all!" one of the guys yelled out. Everybody laughed.

"I wish I could, but the district rules are that I can only have twelve *people* on the squad."

I noticed the way he said the word *people*. Did this mean Tammy was going to make the team?

These last cuts were going to be the hardest. Those first seventeen guys cut would only ever see a basketball game from the stands. How could they be so unaware of how limited their skills were? We all knew the core seven or eight people who were going to be on the team, but the last four spots would be harder to fill—there really wasn't much difference between the remaining players.

My dad had always said that the first few selections for a team were about skill and the final ones were about character. You had to find people who were team players, who could mostly sit on the bench, play hard in practice, feel positive and make a contribution if their number was called.

"The list will be posted on the gym bulletin board tomorrow morning. If anybody has any questions after, I'm willing to discuss in private the reasons you weren't selected. But the list is final. Have a great night, and get home safely."

We all got to our feet and started toward the change room.

"Junior, Jordan and Aaron, could you stay, please!" Coach called out.

"First cuts!" one of the guys yelled out. There was a lot of laughter.

"Actually, I wanted to have a word with my three co-captains. Let's give them a round of applause."

People cheered and slapped us on the back as they walked away. I was happy to be a co-captain but not so happy about who I was co-captaining with. Aaron could play ball, and I thought he'd been working on not being such a jerk, but I still didn't like him.

Tammy came up to Junior and me and waited as others filed away. "He said 'people.'" She smiled. I liked it when she smiled, the way it wasn't only her mouth and her eyes but her whole body that seemed happy. Tammy had been on Coach about not calling us "guys."

"Doesn't mean anything," Aaron said. He'd overheard her.

"I guess we'll find out," Tammy snapped. She gave another one of those smiles to me. "And thanks for helping me run through the drills."

"No problem," I replied.

"You know that was all Jay's idea," Junior said.

She looked surprised. I was surprised too, but I tried not to show it.

"Yeah, I didn't fight it or anything, but he came up with it. I think he wants you to stick around."

Tammy looked embarrassed. I felt embarrassed for her and for me. I had to say something.

"I want the best team we can have. Just trying to do that," I said.

Tammy shook her head and sent her ponytail swinging. She smiled, but it didn't extend through her whole body. "Either way, thanks."

She headed off to the change room—the girls' change room. Soon it was only the three of us standing there. Coach Tanner had taken a seat at the far end of the gym.

"Congrats," Junior said as he and Aaron shook hands.

"Yeah, congratulations," I offered. We shook hands too. I hoped I sounded like I meant it.

"And you," Junior said, pointing at me, "I'm still a little surprised you made the team, so you being a co-captain is actually shocking. This must be like a pity selection because Coach feels sorry for you or something."

"Can you spell 'shut up'?"

"I can spell it, but I doubt I can do it. Aaron, aren't you surprised he's still here?"

"Actually, I'm surprised he isn't the only captain," Aaron said.

I startled slightly.

"I am offended!" Junior said.

"Don't be. Don't get me wrong—you're a great point guard and we're going to be a really good team, but it feels like J.R. is the natural leader here. He should be the captain, and we should be the assistants."

"Thanks, Aaron." No one responded. "I mean it. Especially coming from somebody who knows how to play ball. You know the game. You're going to be a great co-captain."

"How sweet," Junior said. "Do you two want a little time alone, give each other a hug, maybe a little Euro-style kiss on both cheeks?"

"Does he ever shut up?" Aaron asked me.

"I've only known him for seven years. There might have been a time before that when he was quiet, but I doubt it."

"Which is why I should be the only captain," Junior said. "I'm more vocal than the two of you combined."

"Boys!" Coach Tanner called. He gestured for us to join him. We trotted over and sat down.

"I've written down the nine players who are a lock for the team."

He read out the names—the three of us and six other players. There were no surprises.

"What do you think?" Coach asked.

"Good choices," I said. Aaron and Junior nodded in agreement.

"Here's where it gets trickier," he said.

"Or easier," Junior added.

"Easier?"

"Sure. They're not going to get much court time anyway," he explained.

"And nobody left is that much better or worse than anybody else," I added. "They're all pretty much the same."

"One of the potential choices is very different than the rest," Coach said.

"Tammy," I said.

He nodded. "Tell me what the three of you think about her being on the team."

"You want us to decide?" Junior asked.

"No. Ultimately it's my decision. But I do want your input. How do you rank her as a player?"

We all looked at each other. Junior spoke first. "I figure she's probably the tenth or eleventh best player in the gym."

"I've got her at number eight, maybe even seventh. If she were a guy, she'd be on the team for sure," I said.

"But she's not!" Aaron protested. "She's my sister, and being on the boys' team will be bad for her."

"How do you figure that?" Junior asked.

"We're new here, and she already doesn't fit in. Do you think she needs another reason to be different?"

"Boys, could we get back on topic?" Coach said. "She's been really sharp in all the drills, so I know she's coachable."

Aaron opened his mouth to say something but closed it again. He knew we'd been helping Tammy with drills.

"Mrs. Palmerston is going to be coaching the girls' team and told me that if Tammy was on her squad, she'd be the starting guard."

"Which makes sense," Aaron said. "She could be starting on the girls' team and giving them a decent chance at the championship."

I hadn't thought of it that way.

"I don't think she should be on our team," Aaron said. "I vote against it."

"And I vote for it," Junior snapped.

"Do you two think this has become a democracy?" Coach asked. "Neither of you has a vote. I'm asking for your opinions and input before I make the decision. Jordan, what do you think?"

I took a deep breath. I wanted to have a few seconds to think about what I was going to say. "Aaron has a point about her being an asset to the girls' team."

"So you agree with me," Aaron said.

"I didn't say that. Coach, could you sit down with her? Maybe along with Mrs. Palmerston? Tell her how it's going to be, that she's probably only going to get garbage time if she plays with us."

"Garbage time?" Coach asked.

He really didn't know much. "A few minutes at the end of games when it's already decided and things are a blowout. Have Mrs. Palmerston explain to her how much the girls' team needs her and how much time she'll get. Tammy should have a say in which team she wants to be on."

Mr. Tanner chewed on the inside of his lip. "I agree. I'll arrange for a meeting with Mrs. Palmerston tomorrow."

"But aren't you posting the selections tomorrow morning?" Junior asked.

"I'll put up a note saying I'm delaying the decision until the end of the day. And because we don't want anybody to feel bad, this whole discussion has to stay right here, understood?"

"No problem," Aaron said.

"Me neither," I agreed.

We all looked at Junior, knowing that if anyone was going to have a problem keeping quiet, it wasn't us.

"You can count on me. All this gym needs is a few slot machines and a roulette wheel," Junior said.

We all looked at him in confusion.

"What's said in Vegas stays in Vegas, baby." He pretended to zip his mouth shut.

"Hit the showers, guys," Coach said. "We have to be out of the building in less than twenty minutes."

We got into the locker room in time to say goodbye to the last few players getting dressed. Two of them were among the walking dead, but they wouldn't know it until tomorrow.

I sat beside Junior. Aaron plopped down on the bench across from us. We peeled off our shirts. I was so soaked with sweat that it was hard to get it off over my head.

Finally the last of the guys finished dressing, said goodbye and left, leaving the three of us alone.

"She shouldn't be on the team," Aaron said.

"Not our decision," Junior replied.

"But it was your decision to help her with the drills."

"Just trying to make the team better."

"It would be better for her if she didn't make the team."

"How do you figure that?" I asked.

"Like I said, my sister has enough problems fitting in. She doesn't even have other girls to eat lunch with. Look, she's younger than everybody and has always been too smart for her own good, and she's always doing all those protest things. The last thing she needs is to be on the boys' basketball team. She's different enough."

Again, he did have a point. She was already different. This could make her even more different.

"I don't want people to think she's one of *those*."

"One of those what?" I asked.

"You know, a butch."

"A butch?" Junior repeated.

"Do I have to spell it out?"

Junior snorted. "If you're going to be prejudiced, can you narrow it down? Are you afraid people will think she's trans or a lesbian?"

"She's neither," Aaron said.

"But what if she were?" Junior asked. "This is about you and what you're afraid of, not about Tammy."

I nodded my head in agreement.

"Don't pretend you don't know how people are," Aaron said. "You two don't have sisters. Right?"

"We're both only kids."

"I'm her brother, her *older* brother, and it's my job to take care of her."

"She seems to be able to take care of herself on the court," I said.

"And off," Junior immediately added.

"You guys are as bad as Tammy. She's used to a city where people act like it doesn't matter who or what you are, but that's not reality. You don't understand what she's setting herself up for. I don't like seeing her get hurt."

Aaron had twisted his shirt between his hands and was wringing it. He was wrong, but maybe it was for the right reasons. Maybe.

"I understand the taking-care-of-your-family part," Junior admitted. A smile burst onto his face. "If I had a sister, I'd be on her side in every way, every day."

I groaned. Junior's grin broadened. Aaron looked confused.

"Please don't start that again. It's better you shorten words than rhyme them," I said.

Junior turned to Aaron. "You'd never know it, but I used to be quite the poet. I think it shows I'm a natural at spitting flows."

"I'm out!" I said. I kicked off my shorts, grabbed my towel and headed for the shower.

Eight

Aaron put up a shot, and it dropped. The crowd roared. Running back on defense, I looked at the scoreboard. With less than two minutes to go, we were up by twenty-seven points—71 to 44. The only reason they even had that many points was that we hadn't been bothering to play good defense the last ten minutes. That score was actually flattering to them.

Before I could reach our end, there was a whistle. Their coach had called a time-out. Did he really think he had some sort of magical twenty-eight-point play that he'd been saving for this stage of the game? Why not let the clock run out and let us all go home?

I trotted back to our bench. There was a party atmosphere there. Why was it that those who had played the least were celebrating the most? I wasn't going to participate. No sense rubbing our win in the other team's noses. We grabbed our bottles and gathered around Coach Tanner. Coach was pretty happy about how things had worked out. I supposed we all were.

I looked past him to where my dad was, at the far end of the court, up high in the bleachers, standing by himself. I figured my mom hadn't been able to get off work or, more likely, had taken on an extra shift. During every school game the previous year, my dad had been right there watching, most of the time with my mom beside him. Dad didn't like to talk to people during games. He came in right before the end of warm-ups. The coach in him loved watching warm-ups. So did I. When we went to a basketball game together, it was guaranteed we'd be there in the stands long before tip-off.

Dad tapped two fingers against his chest, our sign, and then crossed his forearms over his chest. For a split second it didn't register. Then I realized he was flashing the sign for substitutes. Of course, that made sense. Up this many points with so little time left, why keep the starters in?

"Coach, are you going to put in our second line?" I asked.

Coach Tanner hesitated as everybody looked at him, waiting for an answer. "I was...um...just going to suggest that."

In rapid order he called out five names. Tammy was the first of them. She looked really happy and did that full-body-smile thing. It made me grin. She flashed me a different smile that said *thank you*.

The ref blew his whistle. Aaron, Junior and I, along with the other two starters, headed for the bench while the five players who had been called went first to the scorer's table, then out onto the court.

"Nice call," Junior said as he sat down beside me.

"Just smart."

Junior leaned in closer. "Smart in more ways than one. Did you see the way Tammy looked at you when you suggested it?"

"I was looking at Coach. Now I'm looking at the game."

"And at your father."

"You saw that?"

"Nobody else would even know the sign. I wonder what he thought of Coach's calls all game."

I didn't need to wonder. Coach Tanner didn't know enough about basketball to call plays or react to the other team's plays. We were winning because we were a lot better, not because we were being better coached. Junior and I had worked some two-man plays, but that was it for strategy.

Our opponents brought the ball up the court, and our team settled in on defense. Coach had left them in man-to-man. I would have gone to a zone to make it simpler for five people who hadn't played together. The other team set up the same offense play they'd been running unsuccessfully almost all of the game—a high pick and roll that hadn't been fooling anybody.

And then our coverage broke down, their guard went in for an uncontested layup and our lead was down to twenty-five points.

"Come on, you had to see that one coming!" Aaron yelled from the bench.

"It's okay, bro," Junior said, giving him a pat on the back. "There's no way they're coming all the way back."

The ball was inbounded to Tammy. She started dribbling up the court. Never before had a female player been on the court of any boys' team in the area.

I saw the audience perk up. People were reacting to her being in the game.

Two of the other team's players put on a press. She tossed a long baseball pass over the center line to an open man, instantly and easily breaking the press. Good on her! She crossed half court. The ball came back to her. She was the point guard and was going to run the play. They started weaving, trying to free somebody up. She threw a pass to a back-cutting player—perfect—but the ball bounced off his fingertips and out-of-bounds.

It wasn't her fault, but she was going to get the blame.

This was going to be a long two minutes.

The change room had lots of laughing and joking around. Of course, Tammy wasn't part of the celebrations. She was using the girls' change room.

I changed quickly. I always found change rooms uncomfortable. Maybe being an only child meant I wasn't used to sharing my space, but I really did prefer having my own bathroom and shower and privacy. Of course, Junior was an only child too, and he was comfortable horsing around with the guys.

I pulled my tie on over my head. It was one of my father's. Someday I'd learn how to tie a tie. It was school policy for us to wear a tie, dress shirt and jacket on game days. I didn't mind.

It let everybody know you were part of the team. It was obvious that it wasn't only me who had taken things from a father's closet. There were lots of extra-long ties and baggy borrowed suit jackets. I tightened up the tie. Okay, I was dressed. I wasn't going to stand around any longer. I grabbed my bag and headed for the door. A little quiet time would be more than okay.

As each of my teammates came out of the change room, I said something good about their game and reminded them about practice the next morning. Actually, I was a pretty good captain. Aaron came out and joined me. He had to wait for Tammy the way I was waiting for Junior.

"Easy win," he said. "I hope people know they won't always be that easy. I checked their track record. That team always sucks."

"Your sister did okay."

He shrugged. "That was your father up in the bleachers at the far end, right?"

"Yeah. He doesn't miss many games. Too bad your parents couldn't be here."

"Their commuter train from the city doesn't get into town for another thirty minutes."

Tammy came through the doors. She was also wearing a tie, jacket and a white dress shirt. She was practically swimming in the clothing.

"You know you look ridiculous," Aaron said in greeting.

"Look who's talking. Don't they have mirrors in the boys' room?"

"The girls' team doesn't have to wear ties," Aaron said.

"I'm not on the girls' team. I'm following the boys' team rules."

"Could you follow them a little faster next time? We still have a twenty-five-minute walk ahead of us."

Wait, they didn't have to walk. "Would you like a ride?" I offered.

"Sure. That'd be awesome," Aaron said.

"If that's okay with your dad," Tammy added and gave Aaron a look.

"My dad is always good about driving people home. Of course, since we're waiting for Junior, it might be faster if you walked."

As if on cue, the door opened and Junior walked out.

"Please, no autographs," he said, holding up a hand as if to stop a crowd.

"Hilarious. Every game we've ever played, he's the last one out of the change room," I said.

"You think all this doesn't take time?" he asked incredulously as he gestured at himself.

I was going to say something, but he did look good. His clothes fit right. While most of us had borrowed things, he actually owned a fancy suit and tie. His mother always made him dress up for church every Sunday. He didn't have a dad to lend him stuff, but I doubted his mother would have had Junior looking anything other than polished. Even his hair was slicked and shiny.

Junior looked Tammy up and down. "Tam, you wore that on purpose?" he asked.

"I did indeed, June. It's regulation apparel."

Junior shook his head. "Then wear it on purpose. Do you mind?" Before Tammy had time to protest, Junior popped both the collar of her shirt and suit, rolled the suit sleeves up and folded the arms of the shirt up above her elbows, pulled the tie off Tammy's neck and tied it as a belt. "Now it's got some intention to it," Junior said, surveying his handiwork.

"Whoa," Tammy said as she checked herself out in the mirror at the back of a trophy case. She posed a bit and giggled. "Thanks, June."

"If you're going to stand out, stand out," Junior said. "I can't have everyone on the team bringing down our look like these two." He jerked a thumb toward Aaron and me.

"We're giving Aaron and Tammy a ride home," I said.

"That means you two get to ride in true style," Junior said as he popped on a pair of mirrored aviator sunglasses. "Jay has the sweetest ride in town."

"My *father* has the nicest car."

We circled around the building to the parking lot. It was almost empty. My dad was leaning against the Camaro, arms folded and ankles crossed.

"Really sweet ride," Aaron said low as we headed over.

"The car's got style. So does your father," Tammy commented as my dad stood to his full height.

"Good game," Dad said as we got closer.

"A win is a win. I offered Aaron and Tammy a ride home."

Without hesitation my dad said, "No problem. Hop in, kids."

"Hello, Mr. Ryker. I'm Aaron." He held out his hand to shake. "And this is my baby sister, Tammy."

Tammy glanced fast and hard at her brother before smiling up at my dad.

"Hey, Tammy. Congratulations. First female player on a boys' team in the history of the town."

"And the first one to score points," I added.

"Two free throws when we're up by more than twenty points aren't much to celebrate," she said.

"Yes, they are," my father replied. "There's always pressure coming in late, and you were proving yourself. Lots of history riding on those shots." My dad headed to the driver's-side door.

"Shotgun!" Junior yelled. No point in arguing. He called it, so he'd get it.

We all threw our bags in the trunk before Junior opened the door and pulled the seat forward. Aaron climbed in, followed by Tammy. I climbed in last and plopped down beside her. This was tighter than I'd thought it was going to be. Tammy's leg was pressed against mine. I hunched my shoulders in and stuck my hands between my knees. Now I really wished I'd called shotgun.

My dad started the engine. The car rumbled, then purred.

"This car is really something," Tammy said, leaning forward between the seats. I was grateful, as it gave us some separation.

My dad glanced at us in the rearview mirror. "Thanks. It belonged to my father."

"And someday to Jay Bird," Junior added.

"Jay Bird?" Tammy asked.

He hadn't called me that in years. "Could you go back to

one syllable?" I asked. "Where do you two live?"

"Sixteen Huntington Lane," Tammy said. "Do you know where that is? I can give directions."

"He doesn't need them."

My dad laughed. "I think I know every place there is to know in this town. It's up on the hill in the Ridge Town development. Lots of nice houses up there."

"Big houses," Junior added. "We all call it Rich Town."

"Jordan tells me you moved in before the start of the school year," my dad said.

"Yeah, we moved up from the city," Aaron replied.

"Our parents still work there," Tammy added.

"Going from a city of three million people to a town of one hundred and fifty thousand must be quite a change," Dad said.

"It is. It does feel smaller for sure," Aaron agreed.

"But nice. The people are nice," Tammy added. She had a hand on Junior's shoulder as she continued to lean forward. Was she uncomfortable being pressed against me? Was that why she was doing that? Did I smell bad? I probably did.

"Nicest people in the world in this town," Dad replied. "But you've moved at a weird time. Lots of changes coming with the plant closing down."

"My father said we got our house cheaper because of that," Aaron said.

"More than a little truth to that," my dad replied.

We came to a stop at a red light. A car passing by gave my dad a honk. He waved out the window in response.

Tammy leaned back enough to share a look with Aaron. She rested her hands in her lap as her leg slid against mine.

"How fast can this car move?" Aaron asked.

"The way this one is tricked out, it could probably do close to one hundred and fifty miles per hour," Dad answered.

"Not that any of us will ever see it," Junior said. "Mr. R likes to keep it within the limits."

"Safety first."

My dad revved the engine a little as we waited for the light to change. The engine roared in response.

"No more flutter," Junior said.

"I fixed it. A little adjustment of the carburetor." He revved it again, longer and louder.

The light changed. My dad shifted into first and revved hard, and the car jumped off the line, pushing me back into the seat and Tammy beside me as the tires squealed. He shifted into second and the car jumped again. He took his foot off the gas, and our speed quickly dropped.

"Wow!" Junior screamed. "That was amazing!"

"A little sample of what's hidden under the hood." My dad turned enough so he could see me out of the corner of his eye. "No telling your mother. Tammy, Jordan told me you turned down a starter's position on the girls' team. That must have been hard."

"Not really. It's important for me to make a statement."

My dad nodded. "There are more important things than playing time."

I hadn't expected that from him.

"I'm glad *somebody* understands," she said. I knew she was answering my dad but speaking to her brother.

"Small towns, not small minds. Right, Tammy?" Aaron said as he crossed his arms.

"It's important to stand up for what you believe," Dad said, ignoring Aaron. "It's brave. Good for you."

We turned, passing through big gates and stone walls that marked Ridge Town. We climbed until we reached their street, stopping in front of their house. It was big even compared to the other houses in the development.

Junior got out and held the front seat forward so I could climb out first, followed by Tammy and Aaron. Tammy brushed against me as she passed. She and Aaron said thanks to my dad and goodbye to Junior and me. I climbed back in.

"Aaron can play some ball," Dad said. "He's not bad. Tammy did okay too."

"She's improved a lot, and she's fast," I commented, one knee pressed into the back of my dad's seat and one into Junior's. I leaned forward, elbows resting on my knees.

"They seem like nice kids. Tammy looked cute in that getup," my dad said.

"I'm glad somebody in your family noticed," Junior said.

"I'm sure Jordan noticed," Dad said. "Although it's probably best not to get involved with a teammate."

Junior laughed louder than the joke deserved. "Let's talk more about Tammy and Jay over dinner."

"Sorry, but I'm going to have to drop you off at home. Family dinner tonight."

"What? I'm not family?" Junior asked.

"Of course you are, but it's just immediate family tonight. The three of us. We have, um, things to talk about." My dad shifted in his seat uncomfortably.

I didn't have anything to talk about except today's win, so that meant there were things I had to listen to. Suddenly I wished Junior could be there for dinner instead of me.

Nine

"Good game, man. See you tomorrow," I said to Junior.

"You too. Don't worry."

I knew he was talking about the family "talk." I took over the passenger seat as Junior gave a backward glance and disappeared inside his house. His mom, still in her scrubs, bustled to the door to wave goodbye.

Dad pulled out and switched on the radio.

I reached over and switched it off.

"What's going on?" I asked.

"Jordan," my dad said. "I told you the other night your mom and I would be talking and making some changes. I really shouldn't say any more without her."

He reached for the radio again and turned it back on. It was a short and uncomfortable drive. We pulled into the driveway. I was up the path and into the house before my dad had unlocked the trunk.

"Mom?" I called, heading inside. "Mom?"

I saw her through the sliding doors off the kitchen, flipping burgers on the grill outside. If my mom was barbecuing, it meant she and my dad weren't risking a fight. My dad always wanted to man the grill, but my mom was actually better at it. That would have been enough to set one of them off lately. They must have called some kind of truce.

Mom smiled at me and Dad, although her eyes were red and swollen. Maybe some smoke from the grill had gotten into her face.

"Almost done, boys," she said as she closed the lid.

The table was set with a big salad, a plate of buns that were not homemade—another potential cause of a fight—and most of the condiments from the fridge.

"What's going on?" I asked again.

"Finish up, Mandy," my dad said.

My mom nodded.

I sat at the table and shoved my plate forward.

My dad drummed his fingers on the edge of the place mat. He seemed nervous.

Mom came into the kitchen and put the plate of steaming burgers down in the middle of the table. "Let's eat," she said as she took a seat.

The burgers smelled great, and although I was ravenous, I said, "I'm not hungry. I want to know what's going on."

Mom reached across the table and gripped my dad's fingers, stopping them from drumming.

He looked down at her hand and frowned.

"Your mom and I decided to go to counseling," he said and pulled his hand out from under my mom's as he sat straighter in his chair. "We began discussing how things aren't working anymore."

"But you're going to fix them?" I asked.

"We're going to try our best, but…" Mom started, then caught my dad's eye.

"But it's not an easy fix," he finished. "But we're talking again and trying not to fight."

I looked at my mom and saw her eyes had become even more red.

"Isn't that a good thing?" I asked.

My dad took a burger and placed it onto a bun on his plate. Then he switched plates with my mom and did the same.

"It should be, but it's not going to feel that way," he said. "Living together, our marriage, it's not…I don't know…I need space, Jordan. Your mom and I need space so we're not so angry anymore, so we can be better parents who aren't always fighting over stupid little stuff. There's one more thing that will happen while we're trying to work it out."

"Your dad and I made a decision," my mom said.

"Mandy, you don't need to take the blame on this one." He lifted the top of the burger bun and then dropped it back down. "You should really eat, Jordan."

I ignored his advice and the burgers. "What's the one more thing you decided?"

"If I keep living here, your mom and I will keep fighting and making everything miserable for everyone. I've decided… I'm…I'm moving out."

"We thought it would make the counseling more effective."

My mom reached for my dad's hand again. He let her take it. I stared at her, then him.

"Jordan?" my dad said.

I didn't answer.

"I already found a place with somebody who used to work on the line. She has a space above her garage. One of her kids used to live there. It's in the next town, but it's not far. It's cheap and it'll do for now."

"When will you move out?"

My dad looked at my mom. "I guess as soon as I can get some stuff together," he said. "It'll be a change, but I'm hoping a good one. It's not what any of us want."

"Then don't do it. Stay here and go to counseling and… and…" My words trailed off.

"It's not about what we want but what we need," my dad said.

"And you're all right with this?" I asked my mom.

She hesitated for an instant. "We decided together." I didn't believe her.

I turned to Dad. "What if I say I want to live with you?"

He raised his eyebrows.

"You don't want to live with me?" my mom asked. Her voice quivered, and the tears welling in her eyes finally slid down her cheeks. She didn't wipe them away.

"I didn't say that—I didn't mean that. I want to live with both of you."

"That's not an option," Dad said. "I have to leave and you have to stay. I need to figure this out on my own."

"How do you think going away is going to fix it?"

"Jordan," he said, "as much as you might not want to hear this, I need to be out of the game for a while."

"We'll keep going to counseling and see what type of damage we can mitigate," Mom said with no tone or emotion considering she was crying. "It's only temporary."

"I don't think we can guarantee this is temporary," my dad said, not looking at Mom but at me. "I don't know where we're going to find the money for the extra rent as well as counseling."

"We need the counseling. You agreed," Mom said.

"Because you pushed," Dad said. There was a long pause. "As usual."

As my mom opened her mouth to reply, I shoved a burger between one of the buns and walked away from the table.

Both of their heads pivoted to watch me as I took a big bite and kept walking.

"Jordan, you need to stay for this discussion," my dad said.

I could tell you the same, I thought. I knew better than to say it. "It sounds like you two have figured out what's going to happen. Without me. I'm going to my room."

"You need to sit back down."

"If you get to walk away, why can't I?"

"Sit down and eat some salad."

"Salad?" I laughed. "Seriously? You're checking out of our family, and I should sit down and eat a salad?"

My dad stood up and towered in the kitchen doorway as I reached the bottom of the stairs. "At least finish your burger."

I made a point of shoving the rest of the hamburger in my mouth and turning my hands to show him it was all gone before I put one foot on the first step. I swallowed the barely chewed pieces before I said, "I'm going to my room, but I'm still going to be living here. You're bailing." I could see him almost grow bigger and fill out the doorframe. I wanted to say, I'm the man of the house now, and I don't have to listen to you. But I only thought it.

"Sit back down now, Jordan!"

My mom stood up and held one of my dad's forearms. The tears on her cheeks had dried. "Let him go, Chris," she said quietly. He went to move to the staircase. "Jordie, up to your room. Chris, sit down."

For a second everyone in the house seemed to hold their breath.

"Mandy," he said. It sounded like an explosion was coming.

"I think you were right. We all need some space. I'll help you pack," she said. "To your room, Jordie."

Still framed by the kitchen doorway, my dad crumpled onto a chair. I ran upstairs, three steps at a time.

I could hear them moving around in their bedroom, drawers opening, voices hushed, not much conversation. I heard the front door close, the trunk of the Camaro slam, then nothing.

My bedroom door opened and Mom was there, a silhouette. I turned my head to stare at the wall, my back to her. I didn't really care if she knew I was ignoring her this time.

I heard her move across my bedroom floor and sit on the edge of my bed. She didn't say anything. She gently patted me on the back.

I turned over, and she began stroking my hair.

"I didn't mean to make you cry," I mumbled.

"You didn't. I wasn't surprised when you said you wanted to live with your father. Hearing it though…"

"I've kind of blamed you for all the fighting."

"I knew that," she said. "Ice cream?" She picked a container with two spoons on it up off the floor. I hadn't realized she'd brought that in.

We turned to face each other, sitting cross-legged on my bed as she opened up the container of mint–chocolate chip. My dad hated this flavor. My mom had brought it home for the two of us.

"Tonight wasn't how I wanted things to go for any of us," my mom said between spoonfuls. "Especially for you."

"I didn't think he'd just leave like that," I said.

"This isn't the first time we've separated, Jordie."

"What are you talking about?"

"You were too young to remember," she said.

"But the way you two recite the story of getting together is like some modern fairy tale."

My mom swallowed some ice cream. "We've broken up a few times, but we separated twice after getting married. Once shortly after becoming newlyweds."

I felt the ice cream melt on my tongue.

"He came back because I told him I couldn't go through the pregnancy alone."

I nodded. "He came back because of me then."

Mom dug into the ice-cream container. "No. He came back. I lost that baby."

"I didn't know. I'm…sorry."

"Nothing to be sorry about. There was never a reason for you to know that."

She worked at digging out a deposit of chocolate chips.

"We were both hurting, but I was destroyed. Your dad helped me put myself back together," she said. "It was hard. He stayed when maybe he had no reason to. Then I got pregnant with you, and we ended up separating again for several months. It was before you turned one. We managed to keep it hidden."

"Wait. Why?" I asked.

"This town can be vicious with people's personal lives, and there's nothing much more personal than losing a baby or having a failed marriage. It won't be long before this is being talked about. We're going to have to trust that this is for the best." She paused. "At least for now."

We sat there sharing ice cream and silence. I wasn't sure there was anything more to say.

The ice cream and hamburger felt like they'd formed a solid mass in the bottom of my stomach. I knew she didn't realize it, and she'd meant to comfort me, but my mom had just told me that my dad had practice at leaving me behind.

Ten

The Camaro wasn't in the driveway when I awoke. Somehow I'd thought—or maybe hoped—he'd be back. He'd been packed up and gone before eleven the night before. Only a couple of hours between telling me he was moving out and actually moving out. It was hard to believe any of this could be real, but along with his car being gone, there was something else to confirm it—no smell of baking downstairs.

This wasn't some bad dream. It was real. My father had moved out. I went downstairs and heard the coffeemaker beeping periodically, reminding no one in the room that the fresh brew was ready. I grabbed a box of sugary cereal that Mom kept in the house but Dad wouldn't have wanted us to eat. I stuck my hand into the box, pulled out a fistful of cereal and stuffed it into my mouth. It tasted so good it didn't need milk or a bowl.

"Morning," my mom said as she came into the kitchen. She was in jeans and a T-shirt.

"Hey," I said. "Aren't you going to work today?"

"I'm not scheduled," she answered. "Anything you want to talk about?"

"Nothing." Which really meant so many things that I didn't know where to start or how to say any of it.

"Your dad is coming by later for some more stuff, and we've got a counseling session scheduled after that. Listen, Jordie, I think you'd better tell Junior your dad moved out if you haven't already."

I hadn't texted or called him. I'd picked up the phone to call him half a dozen times the night before and kept putting it back down. It wasn't just with my mom that I didn't know what to say.

"I'm going to talk to Junior's mother about things after her shift tonight, so if it's easier to come from her, it can happen that way," Mom said.

"No, I'll tell him. I thought you two might be keeping it quiet again," I said. I intended to talk to Junior about everything on the way to school, if I could get it out.

"You know there are no secrets in this town. Mr. Kenshaw next door saw your dad loading the car last night and ended up asking him a lot of questions. Your father texted to let me know the cat's out of the bag already."

I put some cereal into a bowl for Mom as she poured herself a cup of coffee.

"I have time, so I can drive you to school this morning if you want," she offered.

"I think I'd rather walk with Junior. I should get going actually."

"Try to have an okay day. If you need to come home, call, and I'll have them sign you out."

I looked over my shoulder at my mom, standing in the middle of the kitchen, staring around and looking confused, cereal and coffee forgotten on the counter.

"Mom? Are you going to be okay?"

"Just fine, Jordie," she said, plastering the too-big smile on her face. "Just fine."

"Are you sure?"

Her face dropped, and she shook her head. "I'm not sure about anything anymore."

"I could stay home if you want."

"I appreciate the offer, I really do, but you need to get to school. That was sweet of you, though." She came over and gave me a big hug, squeezing me tightly. She didn't let go, and I didn't want her to. She needed to give me a hug, and maybe I needed to be hugged.

"That's a lot," Junior said when I had finished telling him. "But it's not like we couldn't see it coming."

"I didn't see it coming."

"What? They've been fighting forever."

"Because it's been forever, I didn't think it would lead to this, to my dad leaving."

"That makes sense. At least they won't be arguing so much anymore."

"I guess," I said. "Listen, don't go telling people, okay?"

"Scout's honor." Junior said and did some weird salute thing.

"You were never a Scout."

"Neither were you. I'd have rocked that little badge-sash-and-neck-scarf thing though." Junior began strutting, very badly, as if he were on a runway.

I began to laugh. Junior could always make me laugh.

"You're an idiot," I said.

"And everyone loves me for it," he shouted over his shoulder.

The day had been long and difficult. I'd been distracted, unable to follow anything in class. Even worse, Coach Tanner had asked what was wrong with me because I'd screwed up a couple of the drills in practice. I'd told him I was just tired. If people at school knew already, nobody was saying anything directly to my face.

My house wasn't far away. I slowed down as I came to the corner. I didn't want to go home. I wanted to keep walking, but there was no place else to go. I turned the corner and saw Dad's car in the driveway. He'd come back! And then I remembered what my mom had said that morning—he was coming over to get more of his stuff. He wasn't coming home, he was moving farther away.

I heard them as I came into the house. I entered as quietly as I could and left the door ajar so they wouldn't hear it close. I stood in the laundry room and watched them. Mom was sitting at the table, a wad of balled-up tissues in her hand, and Dad was pacing the length of the kitchen, which only took him a few strides. The groceries on the counter were spilling out of their paper bags. Neither of them saw me.

Part of me thought I should let them know I was there—yell "I'm home"—but I didn't. I just stood there, invisible, listening, not wanting to be part of whatever was going on.

"It was what they *didn't* say, Chris. And really, you're the last person I want to see or talk to right now."

"That's not fair."

My mom stood up and faced him. "I can't talk to you right now, Chris. I actually can't. First I get grilled in the checkout by the other moms about why I can't make it work with you, and then I actually find out why. And now you refuse to go back to counseling."

"Talk to me, right now. I'm ready to talk."

"I love you, Chris. I love you despite everything. That's what's not fair. So…no, I can't talk to you right now."

"Mandy," my dad whispered. He reached for her.

She jerked away and took a step back. "I *can't*, Chris."

His hand hung in midair, still reaching for her. He closed his mouth and opened it again, like he was trying to say something.

A sudden breeze pulled the laundry-room door shut.

"Is that you, Jordie?" Mom called out.

"Yeah, it's me."

"We're in the kitchen," she said. "Come and join us."

I didn't have any choice. Being invisible was no longer an option. I entered the kitchen. "Hey," I said.

"Your dad came by to get some stuff, and he's going to take you this weekend," Mom said.

"I am?"

"Yes. Your son should see where you're living. The counselor said that was important. You agreed to it. Remember?"

"I agreed he should come over, but I didn't think so soon. I'm not really settled in. Nothing is unpacked, and there's not really..." He trailed off.

"You'll have a few days to figure it out. That's what we agreed would be best for Jordie. And you have to talk to your son. You, Chris. That one's all yours."

"I just need a little more time and space," Dad said.

"Is that what you're calling it? Space?" my mom asked.

He sighed before he said, "I'm sorry, Mandy. I didn't mean to hurt you. None of this was done to hurt you."

"It doesn't matter what you meant to do. You *did* hurt me, worse than anybody ever has."

He opened his mouth again, and I expected him to try to apologize once more, but he didn't.

"You should go now," she said.

"I'll call you later in the week," he mumbled.

"You can do whatever you want." She gave a sad little laugh. "You're going to anyway."

Eleven

My father drove the car the way he always did, deliberately, right at the speed limit, stopping exactly the way he was supposed to at each stop sign. Though I usually found that annoying, today it was almost reassuring—some things didn't change.

It wasn't far from our house to his place, but the drive seemed to take a long time—just like it seemed like a long time between the beginning of the week and this weekend. When he'd picked me up, he and my mom had said few words. They were polite but definitely not friendly. I sensed she was angry that he hadn't kept his word to have me over for the weekend—at least, not the whole weekend. Sunday morning to Monday was part of the weekend, though, and it really wasn't his fault—it was a work thing. He was going to drive me to school in the morning—picking up Junior too—when he drove to the plant.

"Sorry I wasn't able to connect with you as much this week as I would have liked," Dad said.

"That's okay."

He'd been asked to supervise the evening shifts.

"It would have been better to stay on the day shift, but you know when the big boss called and asked if I'd make the move, it really wasn't a choice so much as a polite way of ordering me. I guess I should take it as a compliment, because he knows in all of management, I have the best relationship with the line workers."

"Did it work?" I asked.

"It did. Things are running much better. Just bad timing, as it was this week. I was home when you were at school and at work when you were home. I couldn't be there for you the way I should have been. The way I would have liked."

I almost said something about his leaving home being the problem, not his supervising the evening shift, but I didn't. We both had things we knew better than to say.

"How's your mother doing?"

I almost said Like you care, but this was another thing I knew better than to say. "She's okay, as good as she can be, I guess."

"Has she talked to you more about things?"

"Things?"

"My leaving. The reasons behind it."

I shook my head.

"It was a rough week for everybody. The highlight was getting to see your game."

Dad had left work to see us play. He'd been at his usual

spot up in the bleachers, standing by himself, tapping his chest with two fingers when we saw each other.

We'd won the last game by five points, but I'd had little to do with it. I'd played worse than I could remember ever playing. I couldn't keep my head in the game. Not being able to focus had been my problem all week, but somehow I'd thought my basketball playing wouldn't be affected.

"I hope you've been talking to Junior," Dad said.

"Always."

"It's good to have somebody to talk to."

"He was a little surprised."

"Surprised, huh? I think I surprised a lot of people. Including me," he said. "I'm glad he's there for you."

It *was* good to have Junior. I really didn't have anybody else to talk to about what was going on.

"I know your mom and I could arrange a counselor for you if you want. We'd figure out how to make it work."

I snorted. "You don't even want to go to counseling! You think *I'm* the one who needs it?"

"I didn't mean it that way. I know this is my issue and your mother's. I meant if you did need somebody, we'd arrange it."

"I'm okay. Everything's fine."

We drove along in silence. He knew as well as I did that I wasn't fine.

"Here we are," Dad said.

We pulled up to a big brick house with a large lawn. We rolled down the driveway to the garage. The garage my father was living above. It was hard for that to sink in. This was the place where my father was living. Not our house, not with us, but above a garage, and not even our garage.

An old hoop was above the garage door and below a wide peaked window.

He stopped the car at the side of the garage, by a set of stairs leading up, and turned it off. I grabbed my bag and basketball from the back seat.

"I'm going to pick up a new net," Dad said as we looked at the tattered strings dangling from the rim.

We climbed a flight of splintered wooden stairs with their paint peeling off—only a few flecks still hung on.

"I'll be fixing these. It's not a bad place. The rent is cheap because the owner needs someone to take care of things."

He unlocked the door, and I followed him inside. Other than the washroom, it was one big room, the same size as the garage under it. The ceilings sloped, and there was a small kitchen on the far wall, a mattress on the floor and a few boxes of my dad's clothing stuck in a corner.

"There's a TV behind those boxes. I'm going to have to get a newer one to watch basketball, but I haven't had time. And there's an old video-game console."

I dropped my bag and ball and went to the corner to shove the boxes aside. There was a stack of classic games.

"I don't really have anything to cook or to cook with. I guess we're ordering pizza tonight."

I nodded. We'd never ordered pizza since my dad had started making it. I actually missed takeout pizza.

I poked through the games.

"There's an old NBA game," I said. "You want to be player one or two?"

My dad stretched out on the mattress that we'd be sharing—he barely fit—and picked up a controller.

Dad ordered the food and then we played a few rounds before pausing.

When that game got boring, I switched it out for another. We picked up the controllers, but before the game started, my dad said, "Jordan, you know I love you, right?"

I looked at him.

"You know that? As your dad, I'm always going to love you. You don't have to do anything. I just will. I want you to know that."

"Do you love Mom?"

"Wow, you're driving right to the basket, aren't you?" He paused. "What if I told you I do?"

There was a knock at the door. Dad groaned as he got up to answer it.

"An old lady in the house said this was probably for the guy living above the garage. Tip isn't included," said the guy holding the pizza box.

"I told them it was for behind the house when I ordered."

"It didn't get as far as me," the delivery man said. "Is that your car down there?"

"That's my baby."

"What is it, a '69?"

"You know your cars," my father said.

"I should. My old man used to make 'em."

"He worked at the plant?"

"His whole life. Retired about ten years ago," the man said.

"What's your father's name?"

"Newman. Gus Newman."

"I know Gus. Great guy! I was at his retirement party."

"You work at the plant?"

"Yeah, my whole life too," my father said.

"Sorry about the way things are going."

"Nothing we can do. So how's Gus doing?"

"Not so good. He died three years ago."

"I'm sorry to hear that," Dad said. "I didn't know, or I would have come to the service."

"I appreciate that, but my pops didn't like gatherings. Told us he didn't want anything spent on a funeral."

"That sounds like Gus. Please pass on my condolences to your mom—Mary is her name, right?"

"Yeah, Mary. I will. Thanks. You know, if he wasn't dead already, it would have killed him to know the plant is closing down," the delivery man said. "It was his life."

"It's killing a lot of us. Pretty sad." My father handed him some cash. "Keep the change."

"Thanks. Hey, are you sure? That's a pretty generous tip."

"I'm sure. You take care and say hello to your mother from Chris Ryker."

"I'll do that."

My father closed the door, and we settled in around the counter in the little kitchen.

"It smells good," I said as he opened the box. We both fished out pieces.

"Probably the only thing that's going to smell good in here. I can't see doing much baking. There's no space."

I took a big bite. It tasted as good as it smelled.

"How about after we finish up, we have a game of one-on-one?" I asked.

Dad smiled. "I can't think of one thing in the entire world that would make me happier."

And right then, neither could I.

Twelve

I sat silently while Junior joked around with everybody. He kept things light, and the other team members sitting with us—Donavan, Jing, Evan and Aaron—were enjoying his act. Junior never felt nerves. Sometimes I couldn't decide whether he was fearless or foolish. Either way, I was glad he was on my side—in everything. It felt like he was the only person who was on my side, the only person I could talk to.

I took another bite from my sandwich. I hadn't even touched my fries. I always found on game days that I didn't have much of an appetite. But whether I was hungry or not, I had to eat. Food was fuel, and without fuel the engine didn't run. So I took another bite from the sandwich I'd brought, even though my mom had been slipping me money to buy whatever I wanted from the caf. It was strange that we suddenly had money for lunches now. Still, I missed the lunches Dad used to make for me.

I missed a lot of things. But I didn't miss the fighting. Things felt sad at home, but they didn't feel angry. I didn't have to sit at the table waiting and watching for one of them to throw a grenade at the other. Sad was probably better. At least sad could become happy someday. What had been going on for years really wasn't working, so why not give this a chance? Besides, how long could it be for anyway? He'd told me he still loved her. I was positive she wanted him to come back. They both just needed time to think.

Word had gotten out about my parents' separation. The school principal, Ms. Jones, had talked to me. She and my mother wanted me to know she was "there for me." Like that meant anything. I was sure Coach Tanner knew too. He hadn't said anything, but he had a different tone in his voice these days.

Junior's voice snapped me out of my thoughts. "You're both wrong," he said. "Batman is nothing but a tool belt that would not be allowed on the court. Do you think they're going to let me carry a hammer into the game? Spidey would be the best b-ball player of all the superheroes. The guy has a vertical of, like, a hundred feet, and—" Junior stopped talking and pointed toward the door of the cafeteria. "Is that Tammy?"

I looked where he was pointing. Tammy was in a different homeroom, so we normally didn't see her before lunch. I looked but didn't see her. And then I did. She was wearing a dress. I'd never seen Tammy in a dress before. I didn't think any of us had, except maybe Aaron.

"That's my sister being stupid again," Aaron said.

"'Stupid' isn't how I'd describe her," Junior said.

"I guess I should be grateful she's not wearing a suit today."

We were all, of course, in our game-day gear. We had an away game after school, so all us guys were in our fathers' jackets again. Well, everybody except Junior, who was dressed in his fancy church outfit.

Tammy came toward us, and I saw more of the outfit. The dress was eggplant purple, covered with lace, and it had a mullet skirt—which I knew only because I remembered my mom once telling me that style was called a mullet skirt, and I'd laughed and thought of the dads or moms in town who sported mullet hairstyles. Tammy's hair also looked fancy, and she even had on shoes with a little heel. As she got closer, I could see she was wearing makeup—like, mascara and maybe some stuff on her lips and cheeks. She didn't usually do that, did she? Maybe I hadn't really noticed before.

We weren't the only ones who'd noticed. Heads at other tables were turning as Tammy walked by. She was pretty, especially when she wasn't dressed in sweats. Not that I minded her being in sweats.

A table of girls looked at Tammy, then leaned toward one another and started whispering. I knew the other girls in our class weren't exactly Tammy fans, but they mainly ignored her.

Junior borrowed a vacant chair from the next table and brought it back to ours, shoving me over so he could put it between him and me.

"You are planning on joining us, aren't you?" Junior asked.

"Where else would I sit?" Tammy said as she took the seat and put down her tray.

"It's nice to have somebody else here who knows how to dress for a game," Junior added.

"Likewise," Tammy replied.

"Maybe next time we should all wear dresses," Aaron said.

"Feel free to dress any way you want," Tammy said, "because I will be there to show you support."

Everybody chuckled and looked amused except Aaron.

"What were you talking about?" Tammy asked.

"Spider-Man versus Batman in basketball," Aaron said. "Junior's underestimating Batman."

"How can you even say that?" Junior asked.

"Did you consider they're from different universes? We're talking Marvel against DC, not just Batman versus Spider-Man," Tammy said as she took a sip of water.

"She's smart and can shoot hoops *and* knows comics!" Junior exclaimed. "Working to become the perfect girl!"

"You even got more playing time last game," I said.

"A little. That's not what matters. It's the principle behind it," she replied.

"Playing time is good though. Coach is more confident about having you out there."

"It's encouraging when people believe in you." She looked directly at Aaron and didn't add anything more.

"I'm worried about the energy factor in the last game," Junior said. "We need to get more jacked about today's game. How about I get everybody a little something extra for fuel? My treat. More fries for everybody!"

"Really?" Donavan asked.

"Well, Tammy already has some on her tray, and Jay hasn't eaten the ones he bought. But the rest of you, come on."

Everybody got to their feet. Junior moved to my side, bent down and whispered in my ear. "Hey, buddy, don't do anything I wouldn't do."

I felt my whole body stiffen. They walked away as I prayed Tammy hadn't heard.

"What did he mean by that?" she asked.

So much for prayers. "It's just Junior being Junior."

"Still, I don't get it."

I felt blood rushing to my face and hoped I wasn't blushing. "It's just that Junior thinks I like you."

"Don't you like me?"

"Well, sure, of course."

"Good. Aaron says people don't normally like me." She hesitated. "I like you too."

That made me feel happier than I'd thought it would.

"I'm curious because why *wouldn't* Junior think you like me?" she asked. "Because you think I shouldn't be on the team?"

"Of course not. I told Coach it would be good for you to be on the team," I stammered.

"You did what?"

"Well, he asked my opinion. Me and Junior and your brother."

Tammy's eyebrows shot up. "Aaron wanted me to be on the team?"

I wished I'd just shut up. I didn't want to rat out her brother, but I wasn't going to lie. "Um, Coach asked all of us our opinions."

She pointed at me with her fork. "So you four guys decided to debate my being on the team?"

I gulped. "I swear it wasn't like that."

"It sounds a lot like that." Her fork was still pointing at me.

I hated that fork pointing at me.

I said, "You wanted a shot at the team. The captains and the coach decide the best players to make the team. Not only you. Everybody. We talked about everyone."

"Oh," Tammy said, and she finally lowered the fork. She shifted fries around her plate.

"I'm really glad you're on the team."

"Me too."

I made a mental note to kill Junior, but not until after the game. Tammy and I sat side by side in awkward silence. When were the others going to come back?

"I'm sorry about your parents," Tammy blurted.

"You heard?"

She shrugged. "Small school. Small town. Junior told me, but I already knew. I hope you don't mind he did that."

"It's not like it's a secret."

"When my parents separated, I didn't want anybody to know," she said.

"I didn't know your parents were separated."

"They aren't now. It was, like, three or four years ago. They got back together. My mother told me they needed time apart to realize they should be together." She paused. "They went to see a marriage counselor, even after they got back together. Are your parents doing that?"

I shook my head. I wanted to tell her that my mom wanted to but my dad was reluctant. Maybe if I told him about it working for Tammy's parents, he'd agree to go back to see somebody.

"I know it's hard," she said.

"It's not so bad eating pizza and playing video games all weekend, or my mom slipping me lunch money. There's no more fighting. It's quieter, at least."

"There was a lot of fighting between my parents too."

"My parents were nonstop. What were your parents fighting about?" I asked.

Tammy didn't answer. Instead she looked down at her tray.

"Sorry, it's none of my business."

"No. It's okay. It's kind of complicated and kind of why we moved. One of them was having an affair with a coworker. I don't really want to talk about it anymore." She looked over at me.

"Okay."

We both ate some fries.

She asked, "Do you think my wearing a dress today is stupid?"

"Why would it be stupid? All the girls' teams dress for game days too." Although, from what I'd seen, they never dressed up as much as Tammy had today. She looked like she was going to a party or a wedding instead of a basketball game.

"Aaron thinks I'm doing this to make a statement."

"Aren't you *always* making a statement?"

"Not *always*." She smiled. "But maybe I am. I guess I'm saying that I can be on the boys' team and still be a girl. I don't want to be seen as one of the guys, you know? I can be different but equal."

"Definitely different but probably not equal."

She looked disappointed. "Maybe you've been hanging around with my brother too much."

"No! I meant guys aren't as *good* as girls. Did you know elephant herds are led by the smartest female?" I asked.

"I hope you're not calling me an elephant."

I began stammering.

Tammy laughed. "Can you imagine how much better the world would be if that was the case with everything? Let the smartest lead the way," she said. "I was wondering…we have another away game on Friday."

"Against General Brock."

"And we also have a school dance that night," she said.

"Yeah, that's right."

"The dance doesn't start until seven. So we can probably play and still get back for the dance, right?"

I shrugged. "There should be plenty of time."

"You're going?"

"I'm a team captain. It would look pretty bad if I didn't go to the game."

"I meant the—you're joking, right?"

"If you have to ask, probably not a great joke. I haven't really decided about the dance."

"I'm going." She paused. "You should go too."

Was she asking me to the dance? Or...? The guys came back to our table, knocking into each other, talking and laughing loudly. Thank goodness no answer was necessary right now. When it was only me and Junior, I'd ask him about the dance. Maybe I should go, which meant both of us would go. I looked at Tammy. I'd have to ask Junior what to wear.

Thirteen

The music was loud, the lights were low, and a strobe light was going, but it was still the gym. People stood in a ring around the court and sat in clumps in the bleachers. There were fewer dancers on the floor than there would be players if an actual basketball game were in progress. The scoreboard at the far end still showed the score from our last home game—HOME 72 AWAY 59. It was a school tradition that the last score stayed up until the start of the next game. That was great if you won, but not so great if you lost. So far, including today's away game at Brock, we were six wins and no losses. A perfect start to the season.

There had been plenty of time to finish the game and get back for the dance. It had been another laugher, winning by almost thirty points. I was back on my game, and it felt good to contribute as the leader. Having so much of a lead meant that Coach subbed out us starters for the entire fourth quarter. Aaron, Junior and I sat and watched while Tammy and the others farther down the bench got a chance to play more than a few minutes. They weren't bad, especially Tammy. She wasn't big or strong enough to handle a low post move, but her basketball IQ was pretty high. It was possible she could even get some time when the game was still in doubt.

We'd finished the game, been driven home to shower and change, and arrived at the dance just as the doors were opening. I'd ditched the tie and jacket but was still in a dress shirt, pants and the closest things I had to dressy shoes— my black-on-black high-top basketball shoes. My father had left lots of things behind, including some aftershave that I'd splashed on. Junior had approved the outfit, but not the scent. I was glad I'd fought the urge to splash on more.

The song ended and the dancing stopped. Junior was out there. He'd been up with three different girls. He actually could dance. He waved goodbye to his partner, who went back to the arbitrarily determined girls' end of the gym. Junior was at my side as the next song started playing.

"You planning on dancing?" he yelled in my ear.

"Are you asking me?"

"I'm asking you to not be a chicken and ask Tammy."

Tammy was standing in a group of girls in the corner at the far end of the gym. They were chattering, but none seemed to be talking to her as much as swarming around her. Her dress was yellow like daffodils.

"How do you know she wants to dance?" I asked.

"She's at a dance."

"I'm at a dance, but I don't want to dance."

"If you don't want to dance, then why did you practically beg me to come with you?"

I didn't have an answer to that question.

"She's here, so she wants to dance. It will be with you or somebody else. She's looking way too fine to stand there with a bunch of girls for much longer," Junior said. "Get in there before you lose your shot."

"It sounds like you want to ask her to dance."

"Now that's the smartest thing you've said all night. That's exactly what I'll do."

"What?"

"I'm going to walk over there and ask her to dance unless you're smart enough, and fast enough, to get there before me."

Before I could say another word, Junior turned and started across the floor. I was so shocked that I froze before running after him.

I grabbed him by the shoulder and spun him around. "She's in the middle of a bunch of girls. What if she says no?"

"I will help part the sea of girls. 'Sides, she won't say no. She wants to dance with you."

"How can you be so sure?"

"You're one of the stupidest people I know," he said, shaking his head. He looked disgusted.

"My marks are better than yours," I protested.

"That doesn't make you smarter. Think about it. She practically begged you to come to the dance. She asked twice on the ride home from the game if you were coming. She told you what she was going to wear. She even asked what sort of music you like. Do you need a written invite or what?"

"Written would be good." I paused. "It's just, well, I'm not that good a dancer."

"Oh, you're not good *at all*."

"What?"

"I've seen you dance. Some people bust a move, but with you it's a busted move."

"Gee, thanks."

"It doesn't matter, especially if it's a slow song. You put your arms around her waist, stumble around the floor and try not to let her feel your hands being all sweaty or step on her feet."

My hands *were* sweaty, and I hadn't considered stepping on anyone. I wiped my hands on the back of my pants.

"If you don't ask, you're going to hurt her feelings. She's waiting for you. So what's it going to be? I can still get over there before you."

"I'll ask."

Junior gestured for me to proceed across the floor. I started walking, and he fell in beside me. As we dodged other couples on the floor, Junior did a couple of little side moves. The guy really did have moves. Tammy saw us coming and smiled. The girls with her turned in our direction and smiled too.

"Hey, everybody!" Junior yelled as they opened their little circle and we joined it.

I nodded as they greeted us.

Junior kept talking, and the girls nodded, talked or laughed in response to what he was saying. I wasn't listening so much as trying to look at Tammy without being too obvious. I thought she was doing the same. She really did look pretty. She was definitely the prettiest person I'd ever had as a teammate.

The song ended and suddenly everybody's voice was way too loud for a few seconds, before they adjusted their volume. Another song began. It was a slow beat. I stumbled forward as Junior gave me a little push in the back.

"Hey, Tammy, would you like to, um, you know, dance?"

She nodded as she slid her hand into mine—thank goodness I'd just wiped it off—and led me out onto the floor. There was lots of open space, but she continued to lead me until we came to the cluster of dancing couples in the very center of the floor. Tammy turned to face me, and I slipped my hands around her waist as she put hers onto my shoulders. We started shuffling around. She smelled good. I'd taken a shower and put on that aftershave, but I couldn't remember if I'd put on deodorant. I wondered how long this song was going to last.

"I like this song," she said.

"I don't really know it—wait. I do. My parents like this guy."

"All parents like Bon Jovi," she said. "What did he think of today's game?"

"I didn't even know Bon Jovi was at the game."

"You really do think you're funny. Your father. What did he think?"

As always, he'd been up in the stands, watching.

"He likes solid defense, passing and team play."

"So he wasn't pleased with what he saw today," she said.

"We scored more points than them and we won, but our defense sucked, and there were too many isolation plays."

"Junior sure likes going one-on-one."

I could feel her hands link behind my neck and her breath against my upper lip. I worried it was sweaty too.

"Leave some room for Him." Donavan's mom, one of the volunteer chaperones, walked by and pointed upward.

I knew I was sweating now and could feel myself going red as I took a step back from Tammy.

Tammy laughed. "Please tell me that's just Donavan's mom and not everyone in this town."

"I, um, I don't really know, not everybody," I stammered.

We rocked from foot to foot a bit more in silence until Tammy asked, "When are the tryouts for the boys' travel team?"

"In a month or—you're not thinking about trying out, are you?"

"Don't look so worried. The league rules make it clear that's not allowed."

"You're not going to fight that?"

"I'm already pretty busy between basketball, school and setting up the social justice club. This school is behind in so many ways. I'll try out for the girls' travel team. I really,

really want to be a starter on that team instead of a scrub on a boys' team. I didn't realize how much I actually like being a starter."

"Does that mean you think you should have played on the girls' school team?"

"No. The principle is too important. And I'm getting more time than some of the guys."

"You're better than most of the guys. My father said that too."

"That's sweet of him. How's he doing, you know, with the separation and all?"

"Better. I'm going to be spending the weekend at his place again."

My mom, on the other hand, wasn't doing so great. Her phone rang a lot, but she didn't answer most of the calls. Any questions I asked about her and my dad, she said he and I needed to talk. But overall she wasn't crying as much now, and when she and my dad saw each other, they were polite. Really polite.

"Does he live close by?"

"Not far. Just in Ajax, the next town over. He's coming to get me at the end of the dance to drive me there. How are you getting home?"

"My mom is picking up me and Aaron."

The song ended. I almost let out a sigh.

"Thanks for the dance," I said.

The music started up again. A fast song.

"I love this song!"

She started dancing. I didn't really have a choice. I shuffled along with her.

We were getting close to the last dance of the night. I'd danced a dozen songs or more—all with Tammy—and probably worked up more of a sweat than I had during the basketball game. The current song was long and hard to dance to. Why was it that "Stairway to Heaven" was still being played at the end of every school dance? My dad told me they played it when *he* was at school. Not that I didn't know and like it. Led Zeppelin was standard music in my father's car. It was a much better driving song than it was a dancing song. Without thinking, I started to sing along under my breath.

"Wait. You know this one?" Tammy asked.

"From my dad. It's sort of a classic. I'm surprised you know it."

She sang the next line. "One of my father's faves too. Classic rock is called classic rock for a reason."

"Especially around here," I said.

"At least it's not country. This whole place seems like it's thirty years behind the city."

"Only thirty?" I joked. "Do you know that some of the words of this song were inspired by—"

"*Lord of the Rings*," she finished.

"Yeah, I love *Lord of the Rings*."

"Me too. I've probably read the whole series five times."

I held up three fingers. "Last year Junior and I did a *Lord of the Rings* movie marathon. We watched all of them, back to back to back."

"That would have taken all day," she said.

"The movies run eleven hours and twelve minutes. Plus we needed bathroom and snack breaks. We sat on the couch for thirteen hours straight."

"That's intense. The movies were great, but of course the books are better."

"That goes without saying," I replied.

"Favorite character?" she asked.

"Well, I really like the Ents."

"They're pretty good, but is there one character?"

"Aragorn."

"He's one of my favorites too. You sort of remind me of him."

"I do?"

"He's the leader. Sort of the captain of the team. Calm, always in control."

"Thanks. I guess that makes you Arwen."

"That's quite a compliment, to be compared to the half-Elven daughter of Elrond and Celebrian."

"You really know your *Lord of the Rings*."

"Aaron says I'm a nerd."

"Your brother's an idiot. *Lord of the Rings* is the best."

"Agreed. We have a lot in common," Tammy said.

I swallowed. "It seems so."

"Basketball, music, *Lord of the Rings* and the fact that we both think my brother is an idiot."

"He's not all bad."

"Wait until you get to know him better." She leaned slightly back so she could look right up at me. "I'm wondering, do you think I'm Arwen because I look like Liv Tyler or because Aragorn has a crush on her and I just compared you to him?"

My brain slipped into mushy overdrive. Tammy must have noticed, because she laughed as the music rushed into the gigantic solo. As guitar filled the gym, Tammy let go of me and began strumming an air guitar, tossing and flipping her hair. I looked around at the faces. Other kids' mouths dropped open. Tammy didn't care what they thought. I shrugged and began smashing away on my air drums alongside her. I wasn't going to care either.

"'And as we wind on down the road, our shadows taller than our soul'!" we both yelled out in unison with the music. Tammy put one hand in mine.

We kept singing, line by line, as other kids on the dance floor looked at us like we were crazy. Tammy grabbed my other hand and started to jump. I grinned at her and began bouncing too.

The drums kicked in. I let go of her hand and hit my air drums until the music slowed. She kept bouncing up and down and tossing her hair. I grabbed both of her hands and pulled her close for the final line.

"'And she's buying a stairway to heaven,'" we sang into each other's ear.

"I warned you two to leave some room." Donavan's mom

reappeared like some sort of Ringwraith. "And to a religious song, no less."

We erupted in laughter, Tammy's arms still around my neck and mine on her waist.

Then it became quiet, and I didn't know what to do with my hands. I really should have let Tammy go, but I didn't. I worried I was making things weird by still holding her when there was no music, so I went to take my hands away.

But Tammy asked, "The dance isn't over, is it?"

I shook my head. "I don't know. It could be."

"And now for the last song of the evening," announced the DJ, a kid who'd graduated from our school a couple of years back.

The music came on. I recognized it immediately. "Perfect," by Ed Sheeran.

"I love this song," Tammy said.

I didn't let go of her. We started to sway. Her head rested on my shoulder. I put my head against the top of hers. She still smelled good. Like fruit or flowers or something.

I saw Donavan's mom out of the corner of my eye, but she smiled, pointed two fingers at her eyes and then at me.

I didn't know what to say to Tammy, but maybe I didn't need to say anything. I listened to the lyrics. This was probably the best song to end the night on. I found myself singing along softly. I didn't know all the lyrics the way I knew "Stairway," but I knew enough. Wait, would Tammy think I was singing to her? I didn't care.

We were coming to the last few notes. The night would soon be over and I'd be going home and I wouldn't be holding on to Tammy and I didn't want the song to end.

Tammy pulled back and looked up at me. She gulped hard, then bit her bottom lip before she said, "You should do it. If you want to, that is."

"I should do what?"

Tammy turned visibly red even in the dim lighting. She pulled away.

The song ended, and I realized what she meant. I tilted my head to the side. I worried that my breath might be bad or taste funny, my lips might be dry or I'd have too much or too little spit in my mouth. Maybe my hands would be sweaty or I'd do it wrong or…I closed my eyes and leaned in, found her lips with mine. They were soft, sliding smoothly, our noses bumping gently into each other. She exhaled, and I breathed it in. One of her hands slipped from behind my neck and gripped the front of my shirt. We kissed for probably only a few seconds. But we kissed. My first kiss.

Donavan's mom grabbed us by the shoulders. "I warned you two!"

A bunch of people began cheering. Tammy ducked out of Donavan's mom's grip and darted out the gym's fire doors.

Junior appeared beside me. I looked down and saw I was standing at center court, my spot.

"Go after her!" he said into my ear. "Now!" He pushed me. I stepped forward, then ran.

I went out the same doors into the parking lot and got there just in time to see Tammy getting into the back of a black car. Aaron looked over the roof as he got in. We locked eyes. He glared at me before he got in too.

I stood staring at the car as it pulled away. Tammy came into focus in the rear passenger window. She brushed her hair away from her forehead, blinked and gave that full-body smile to me.

Junior, out of breath, ran up behind me, arriving just as my dad pulled up in his Camaro.

"Dude!" Junior said as he hopped up and down, almost dancing. "O M freakin' G! That was next level!"

"Shotgun," I murmured as I reached for the door handle.

"Mr. Ryker," I heard behind me and turned to see Donavan's mom over my shoulder. "We need to talk about your boy."

Fourteen

Not only did I have to sit silently while Donavan's mom recounted the night, but then, as we drove, I had to listen to Junior retell his version of events to my dad.

"If it weren't for yours truly," Junior concluded, "none of tonight would have been possible."

Stopped at a red light, my dad glanced at me and smirked. The last thing he had said was when he told Donavan's mom, "It sounds like two kids shared an innocent kiss, but I'll talk to Jordan."

Junior continued, "He was a boss. Beating on his air drums, holding her against him, leaning in and planting one on her."

"It really wasn't like that," I said quietly, slouched in my seat.

"That's enough now, Junior," my dad said, smirking again out the windshield.

"If you had been there, Mr. R—"

"Then I'm sure Jordan would be even more mortified."

Junior leaned forward and punched me lightly in the back of my shoulder. "So are you more a Led Head or an Ed Head now?"

"You going to explain that to me?" Dad asked.

"He was dancing and going crazy when Led Zeppelin started playing, but the kiss was because of Ed Sheeran," Junior explained.

"The Zeppelin makes me proud, but I heard there's a term for Ed Sheeran fans," Dad said. "They're called Sheerios."

"Dad! How would you even know that?"

"I'm old, not dead."

My dad and Junior began laughing and stopped only when we pulled up to Junior's house a few moments later. His mom had probably fallen asleep on the couch, waiting for him.

I hopped out and released the passenger seat. It jolted forward.

"Such a Sheerio," Junior said. He and my dad started laughing all over again.

Once Junior was inside his house, Dad pulled away, still chuckling.

"Do you two have to ruin this?" I asked.

"Did we actually ruin it? It sounds like you *made out* pretty well."

I rolled my eyes. "Busting out the dad jokes now?"

"You have to admit, the whole thing is kind of funny."

"To all of you who didn't have their first kiss tonight," I said.

"I was thinking more of Donavan's mom's reaction," Dad said, all serious. "The more important thing, how was it?"

"Do you really think I want to talk to my dad about this?"

"Fair enough."

I stared out the windshield and thought about Tammy, the way she smelled, the way her lips slid against mine.

"It was good. Really good," I said. Then I remembered the nerves and the other thoughts about bad breath and sweaty hands and doing it wrong. "Mostly good. Can I ask you about this, or are you going to make it weird?"

My dad pulled over. We were only a few streets from home—my home anyway.

"You have my undivided attention and my sincere promise that I will try not to make it weird. But you should be prepared, because these types of talks are always at least a little awkward."

I bit the inside of my bottom lip. "Fine. But try really hard," I said. "I guess I have some questions."

"Okay."

"Do guys normally have a lot of thoughts before kissing? Or is it a first-kiss thing?"

"What kind of thoughts?"

I poked the toe of my sneaker at the edge of the floor mat. "About how things could go wrong."

"Like kissing wrong? Jordan, there's no real right way to kiss. You kind of figure out the other person and whether you both like what's going on as you do it. There's no science or technique."

"Not just kissing wrong. Like, if your breath is fresh and stuff."

Dad turned in his seat toward me. "First kisses are supposed to be nerve-racking, especially if you like the person. It's totally normal to have those thoughts and worries. Once things start, they'll fade away. And once you've had a few kisses, it gets easier."

"So you had those thoughts before you first kissed Mom?"

"More during. I didn't know if I was doing it right."

"But you'd kissed other girls before."

My dad shifted in his seat, turning away from me.

"You already told me you'd kissed other girls before Mom. It's not some big secret."

"Jordan," my dad said, "I'm not sure this is the right time."

"For what?"

"This conversation," my dad said.

"Oh."

"We should get back to my place."

Strange how he wanted to talk about it, then didn't.

He started the engine and went through his checks before he pulled away from the curb. We stopped at the stop sign. I counted to three. We passed by the turn to our old home. It felt wrong.

"How long do you think you and Mom are going to stay separated?"

My dad heaved out a breath.

"Tammy told me her parents separated, but they got back together after a while."

"Your mom and I aren't going to get back together," he said, gripping the steering wheel tighter.

"But Tammy's parents did a bunch of counseling, then got back together and did some more. Maybe you two should really give it a good try."

"The counseling isn't going to help."

"If you don't go, it won't," I said. "I overheard you and mom last week. I tried to ask her about stuff, but all she says is you and me have to talk first. What do we have to talk about?"

Dad signaled and pulled over again, bringing the car to a stop. At this rate we'd never get to his apartment.

"We're not Tammy's parents. Our issues aren't theirs. Your mom and I aren't getting back together, not even if we got all the counseling in the world."

"But why?"

"Because I'm tired, Jordan," he said. "I'm tired, and I can't lie."

I turned sideways in my seat and tucked a leg up under me. "Lie?"

"I'm going out with somebody," he said. He dropped his hands onto his lap and looked at them.

I swallowed, then said, "Tammy's parents got back together after one of them cheated."

"I didn't cheat," he said. "I wouldn't cheat."

"It's only been a couple of weeks since you moved out. If you just met this woman recently, it's not serious then."

Dad looked up at the ceiling. "Even if it's not serious with this person, it's still serious. Your mom was the last girl I kissed. She was also the first."

"But you said—"

"I said she wasn't my first kiss."

"But—"

"I don't want to lie to you." He continued to stare at the roof. "This is so tough." He laughed. "So tough," he repeated, not laughing. "Jordan, I'm seeing another man."

"What? What did you say?"

I stared at him as he looked up at the roof. He closed his eyes and kept them closed. His Adam's apple bobbed as he swallowed and opened his eyes again. He sat up straighter in his seat and turned to look at me.

"Jordan, I'm seeing a man." He took a stilted breath. "I didn't want to tell you this way."

My throat got really dry. "How did you plan to tell me then?"

"I don't know. I ran through, like, dozens of scenarios. I figured if I hadn't by the end of the weekend…"

We watched one another and a million thoughts flooded my mind. He hadn't really said that. Had he? He was my dad, my sometimes coach, my basketball-playing, car-making, Camaro-driving father, who towered above the other men in town and who was recognized everywhere, who drank beer and cheered at all my games and painted a regulation key on the driveway. My dad who didn't dress particularly well or know any current music if I didn't play it for him. My dad who was seeing another man, whose first kiss was with a guy, who had moved out and left my mom and me. Suddenly, somehow, he didn't look so tall or so big sitting in the driver's seat across from me.

"Drive me home," I said.

"What?"

"I want to go home." Neither of us moved, so I repeated, "I want to go home."

He did all his adjustments and checks and signals before he performed a three-point turn and headed back, turning down the streets until we pulled into the driveway. He stopped under the basketball hoop.

The moment the Camaro was parked, I was out of the car. I pulled the spare key from the hiding spot inside the porch light, unlocked the door and entered the house.

My mom jumped off the couch, turning to face the door.

"Jordie, you scared me," she said as she came into the entryway. "What's going on? You're supposed to be with your father."

He entered the house behind me. She looked from me to him.

"Oh," she said.

"Yeah," he replied.

I was partway up the stairs before my dad caught my arm. "Are you mad at me?"

I tried to pull my arm free. "I don't know. I went from having my first kiss, which was mostly amazing, to my dad telling me...telling me..." I couldn't even find the words to say it.

"I have to live an honest life, Jordan. What kind of father am I, what kind of example for you, if I don't?"

"So our lives are a lie. 'Cause you *did* lie, Dad."

My father dropped my hand. "I spent most of my life trying to lie to myself," he said. "I doubt that makes you feel any better. But there it is."

Mom carried a box of extra linens out to the Camaro and put it in the trunk alongside some of dad's cooking gear.

I could see them out on the driveway from where I sat on the stairs. Where my mother had told me to sit.

She leaned up and kissed my dad's cheek, then walked back toward the house. She turned and called to him, "Drive safe."

I must have been giving her a look or something when she came into the house.

"What?" she asked.

"How are you okay with him or any of this?"

Mom went into the kitchen, and I followed. She pulled a bottle out of one of the cupboards. She poured herself a drink in a coffee mug and downed it all in one go.

"I'm not. But I've had a couple of weeks to try to make sense of it. I'm still so far from okay," she said. "I'm angrier at him than I've ever been, and sadder, and disappointed, and a whole heap of other things. And deep down, buried under all that, I'm more worried about him than I've ever been."

"He lied to us," I said.

She lifted the bottle to pour another drink, then recapped it and put it back in the cupboard. "It's too easy to make this all about you or me, Jordie. We talked on the driveway a little.

I realized that, no matter what, he's always going to be your father. He's always going to be part of our lives. We both thought it's better you know before the gossip mill starts."

Gossip—I hadn't even thought of that. What were people going to think? What were they going to say?

"Why are you defending him," I asked, "after all this time you've spent fighting with him?"

She took her coffee mug to the sink and washed it out. "I don't think I am," she said. "I'm struggling but trying to understand what he's been going through."

She sat down across from me. "Did I hear right? Did you have your first kiss tonight?" She smiled. "I suppose you don't want to tell me about it, do you?"

"Nope."

"Then let's try to get some sleep. When I thought you were going with your dad for the weekend, I picked up more shifts. You should call Junior to come over tomorrow. You shouldn't be alone. You can talk to him about…things. You are going to talk to him, right?"

Of course I was. Everything. I'd always told him everything. But how could I tell him this? I'd find a way.

Fifteen

When I heard Mom up early getting ready for work, I rolled over and sandwiched my head between my mattress and the pillow. I didn't want to talk to her right now.

I knew she'd checked on me during the night. When I got up to use the washroom, my door was ajar. It felt like I'd spent most of the night tossing and turning. I'd had weird dreams about kissing Tammy to Led Zeppelin, both of us dressed like elves, at my parents' wedding. Instead of vows, they'd recited the "Ring Verse." I'd woken up as my dad took the priest in his arms and dipped him.

I jumped at the sound of banging against my bedroom wall. I quickly figured out where the noise was coming from, got up and looked out my window. Junior was standing in the driveway. There was another boom as he tossed the basketball against the outside wall of my bedroom. I opened the window.

"What do you think you're doing?" I yelled as the basketball hit the wall beside me again, then bounced back into

Junior's hands. His mom was in her car on the road. She honked twice and waved before she drove away.

"Getting your attention. The spare key isn't in the normal spot, and you weren't answering the door," Junior called up. "Get your butt out of bed and let me in."

I pulled on a pair of sweats and headed downstairs to unlock the front door. Junior was inside almost as soon as the door was open.

"Think fast!" he said, pretending to throw the ball right at my face.

"You could have broken a window."

"Like I would have missed? You look like crap and your breath stinks. Man, I miss your dad's morning baking," Junior continued as he walked into the kitchen. "His bagels were epic, the whole kitchen filled with steam. The best bagels I ever had."

"Well, he's not here," I said. "Nobody's here, if you haven't noticed."

"Someone got up on the wrong side of the bed," Junior said. He took some store-bought bread and put four slices in the toaster.

"And someone didn't help that by smashing a ball into my wall."

Junior shrugged. "Then get your lazy butt out of bed earlier. Or were you tired from dancing with Tammy all night? This is for you, by the way."

Junior tossed something at me. I caught it in both hands. A tube of lip balm.

Junior wiggled his eyebrows and grinned.

"How are you so annoying so early?" I groaned.

The toast popped. Junior juggled the hot pieces from hand to hand. "Some guys get all the gifts, I guess. I know how to make eggs, if you want. Let's get you going so I can wipe the driveway with you."

"I don't feel like playing today."

"You always feel like playing. You mean you don't feel like losing. Can't blame you."

"Stuff happened last night after the dance," I said.

Junior buttered the toast and slid the plate over to me. "Your parents weren't mad about you kissing Tammy, were they? Wait, you're supposed to be at your dad's. Are you grounded?"

"No," I said around a mouthful of toast, crumbs spraying in front of me. "My parents aren't getting back together."

"They're getting a divorce?"

"Probably. We didn't talk about that."

"Half the kids in our school have divorced families. It's no big deal."

I wondered what to say next. How could I say it? Then I wondered if this was how my dad had felt the previous night—and many times before then. I decided to blurt it out rather than think about any of that.

"My dad told me the reason they're not getting back together is because he's dating somebody else."

Junior stopped eating his toast. "Whoa. I have to admit I didn't see that coming. At least, not this fast. I guess it was going to happen sooner or later for one of your parents." He started eating again.

"It's a guy."

Junior stopped chewing. "What?"

"A guy. My father has a boyfriend."

"And you say my jokes are bad."

"I'm not joking."

He looked right into my eyes like he was trying to read me. He dropped his piece of toast back onto the plate.

"You're saying your dad is gay? No way. I don't believe you."

For a split second I thought Junior was right—that it wasn't really what my dad had told me.

"It's the truth. My dad likes guys now."

"Now? But…" Junior began. "Wait, was he seeing this guy behind your mom's back? Like, on the down-low? I didn't think your dad would do something like that."

"Jeez. I don't want to be thinking about my dad cheating on my mom with another guy. Thanks, Junior."

"You'd have gotten there eventually," he said. "I didn't think your dad would have cheated though."

"He said he didn't. I don't know what to think."

Junior finished his piece of toast and took another. "What's so wrong with your dad seeing someone else? I wish my mom would."

Junior's mom had been single since his dad passed. She still often wore dark clothes when not dressed in her hospital scrubs.

"Didn't you hear what I said? He's not seeing somebody else. It's some *guy*."

"I heard. What's so wrong with that?"

"What's wrong with it?" I asked. I felt stunned.

"Everything is what's wrong with it. It's only a matter of time before all anyone is talking about is my gay father."

Junior popped more toast in. "Your dad might be bi or something."

"He kissed a guy before he was with my mom," I said. "And if he's seeing another guy now, he's gay."

"Maybe. There are other gay guys in town," Junior said. "The man who owns the florist shop and has the poodle."

I rolled my eyes. "And who has that voice and talks with his hands."

"The Bianchis all talk with their hands."

"They're Italian, and this is Franklin. Even the flower guy doesn't live in Franklin. And the flower guy isn't my dad!"

"So are you mad 'cause everyone is going to know your dad is gay or 'cause he didn't figure it out sooner?"

I gritted my teeth. "I don't think you understand."

"Then lay it out for me," Junior said. "The problem is?"

"Problems. First, my dad left us."

"Which sucks, but it's only geography."

"He just sprang it on us."

"Did you want him to keep it from you?" Junior asked.

"Of course not. Well, why couldn't he have waited a bit longer before he started seeing somebody?"

Junior shrugged. "It sounds like he waited his whole life. Isn't that long enough?"

I hadn't thought of that. I didn't have an answer.

"Look, your dad is amazing. Moving out and being with another man is big, I'll give you that, but it's not the end of the world. It's not even really about you."

"We're in Franklin," I repeated. "My mom already came home crying because some other moms at the grocery store wanted to know what she did to make my dad leave. Wait until they hear this."

"Then maybe you should stop for a second and consider how your dad might get treated."

"You don't understand. This isn't happening to you."

Junior picked up his basketball. "It doesn't sound like it's happening to you either."

"It *is* happening to me. It's my father. My family. He left us. And he's gay or something. What don't *you* understand?"

"I understand everything. It's you that's having trouble."

"I thought you'd be on my side."

Junior shook his head. "I'm so much on your side right now, you don't even know it. If you don't want to play and would rather sit around feeling sorry for yourself, then I'll leave you to it. I'm heading home."

He walked out the front door, and I didn't stop him. I threw the leftover toast in the garbage and went back to bed, but I couldn't get back to sleep.

I got up again, brushed my teeth and showered. I picked out a nicer pair of jeans and a polo shirt, then put on my fancy basketball shoes from the night before. I hopped onto my bike and pedaled toward Ridge Town. Maybe somebody else would understand.

Sixteen

Nothing was that far in Franklin, but Ridge Town was at the far end of the city, and it was uphill most of the way there. My phone was in my pocket. I could have called, but I wanted to talk face-to-face. I'd ignored the calls and texts from both my mom and my dad from earlier in the morning. I should have at least sent a text back to my mom to let her know I was all right. I didn't care if my dad wanted to talk or give me a call. I had nothing to say to him. It wasn't just that I was angry or upset. I also had no idea what I was supposed to say, and I didn't want to lie and tell him everything was fine when it wasn't. I wanted him to know we weren't okay.

My phone pinged again. I pulled over to the side of the road and took it out of my pocket. I was hoping it was Junior. I did want to talk to him, but I didn't want to be the one who made contact first. Just another message from my mother. She deserved some sort of answer. I tapped out **riding bike. home later** and pushed the Send icon. She didn't need to know where I was riding to. That was my business. People had been keeping secrets from me. Why shouldn't I keep secrets from them?

I put my phone on silent mode and started riding again. If nothing else, I'd caught my breath.

Passing through the big stone gates, I felt less brave. These were big, fancy houses. I'd spent almost no time in this part of town. I felt like I didn't belong. I pictured people peeking out windows, asking, Who is that? and Why is he here?

Coming up to Tammy's house, I slowed down. There were two cars in the driveway, so I knew somebody was home. I passed the driveway and kept going, doing a circle on the street two houses down before coming back toward her house. I rode onto her driveway and did a couple of tight turns, fighting the urge to take off. Did she want to talk to me? What exactly did I want to say to her? If I knocked on the door, would she answer or would her parents?

"Hey, Jordan!"

I was startled out of my thoughts. Tammy stood at her open front door. I wheeled up the driveway, past the two cars, and came to a stop on the walkway in front of her. Her feet were bare. She was wearing jean shorts and an oversized hoodie.

"I just came to say hi."

"Hi." Tammy did that smile that went through her whole body. I felt it spread into mine. "Do you want to come in?"

"No. I mean, sure, if that's all right."

"Why wouldn't it be all right?"

I got off my bike, letting it drop as I followed her inside.

"Do you want something to drink or eat?" she asked.

"That would be good, thanks."

I trailed after her down the hall into the kitchen. A woman was sitting at the table, glasses on the end of her nose, typing at a laptop. She looked like a grown-up version of Tammy. She stopped and smiled when we walked in.

"Mom, this is Jordan."

"Good to meet you, ma'am."

"Very polite! And you. I've been hearing about you."

"You have?"

"You're in eighth grade, do well in school and are the captain of the basketball team."

"*Co*-captain," I said. "Along with Junior and Aaron."

"That's right. Aaron mentioned that, but he also said you were really the captain."

"We're all captains, but that was nice of him," I said.

She turned to Tammy. "You see, your brother can be nice sometimes."

Tammy held up her hands in surrender, then shoved them in the pouch of her hoodie.

"I wanted to tell you how sorry I am about your parents," Tammy's mother said.

"Um, thanks." I wished that Tammy hadn't talked to anybody about—

"That came from Aaron too," Tammy said.

"Speaking of Aaron, let me get him." Her mother moved to the doorway. "Aaron, you have company!" she called.

Tammy and I exchanged looks as Aaron entered the room.

"Look who's here to see you," their mother said.

"Hey, Aaron."

He turned to his mother. "I don't think Jordan's here to see me, Mom."

"Why else would he... " She stopped and looked at Tammy, who stared at the floor. I offered a weak little smile. "Ah."

This was even more embarrassing than I'd anticipated.

"Maybe we should leave you two alone," their mother said.

"Maybe we *shouldn't* leave them alone!" Aaron protested.

"Is there something I need to know?" their mother asked.

"It's no big deal. We danced together," Tammy said.

Their mother said, "That's what happens at a dance."

Aaron looked like he was going to say something, but didn't. I was thankful for that.

"I should probably get going."

"Are you sure you don't want to sit down and have a drink or a muffin? They're homemade banana–chocolate chip, just out of the oven."

"Thanks, but I better get going."

"You could take one for the road. I'll pack a couple."

"Thank you, ma'am."

"The kids in Franklin have such good manners." She looked at Aaron before she put some muffins into a bag and handed them to me. They were still steaming and fogged up the plastic.

"I'll walk you out," Tammy offered.

"Thanks for the muffins."

"You're more than welcome. Drop in anytime. It's always good to have Aaron's, and Tammy's, friends over."

Tammy closed the door behind us as we walked over to my bike. I picked it up and climbed on.

"That was embarrassing," she said.

"A little."

"A lot. Sorry about that."

"You didn't do anything wrong."

"Neither did you," she said. "At the end of the dance, I mean. Sorry I hurried away. I was feeling…uncomfortable. I didn't know what to say to you."

"I didn't mean to make you uncomfortable. I'm sorry. I shouldn't have done it."

"That's not what I mean. I wanted you to kiss me. I told you to. It was everyone watching and Donavan's mom and, maybe, it was me. Are you actually sorry we kissed?"

"Um…I don't know. I guess it was a mistake?"

"You think kissing me was a mistake?" She shifted her weight.

"I didn't mean that. I don't want you thinking I do things like that all the time."

"Do you think I do?" she asked.

"No, of course not."

"Because I don't. You're only the second guy I've ever kissed."

"Second?" I held one finger up then pointed it at my own chest.

"Oh! I'm the first girl you've kissed?"

I nodded. "Kissed that way."

"You kissed good for the first time."

"Thanks."

"Not that I've kissed a lot. I sort of had a boyfriend before we moved."

"That would have made moving here harder."

"No, we broke up before that. He said that I liked whales more than him."

"Okay, I'm confused."

She laughed. "He didn't like my causes. He thought it took time away from him, and he said I was always angry at the world."

"He sounds like a jerk."

"Hopefully my second boyfriend will be better."

"I'm sure he will. Oh. You mean me?"

"I don't go around randomly kissing people."

"So, well, I guess you're my girlfriend?"

"You guess?" she asked. "If you don't want to be, it's okay."

"No! I mean, you are. We are."

"You may have to be a bit quicker if we're going to be together."

I spun the pedal of my bike.

"Did you ride here all the way from your father's place?"

"No, our house. Here in town," I said.

"But weren't you supposed to be staying with your father this weekend?"

"Things changed. He told me some stuff."

Tammy stuffed her hands into her hoodie pouch and waited, flexing her toes between the blades of grass.

I stood there going through my brain, trying to figure out what to say and how to say it.

"It's okay if you don't want to talk about it," Tammy finally said.

"He stopped going to counseling."

"My father didn't want to go either."

"There's more. He said he went out with somebody else."

"That sucks. It still could work out. He might come back."

I could have explained to her she was wrong. I could have told her. I didn't. It was my father—my *father*! If I told her, it would make him different and, somehow, make me different.

"I don't think so," I said instead. "I better get going." I went to start pedaling.

Tammy grabbed my handlebars. We stared into one another's eyes. My face got all warm. She blinked as if in slow motion, then leaned in close. She kissed me, softly, almost like when she brushed past me getting out of the back seat of my dad's car.

"It's okay. Whatever happens will be okay."

My face stayed all warm. "I guess."

She let go of the handlebars and bit her bottom lip.

"See you at practice," I managed to say.

"That sounds so strange." She laughed. "Who would have thought I'd be kissing my teammate?"

"Not me. I really better get going." I grinned at her, and she grinned back.

I pushed off and started pedaling down the driveway. I hit the street, and the slight grade helped me pick up speed. I smiled and felt it spread through me the way Tammy's did, from my mouth, through my chest and out into my limbs. I stood up on my pedals and glided along the street. The ride back home—and downhill—was going to be easy.

Seventeen

A truck I'd never seen before was parked in our driveway. It was a beauty. Dark red like a nosebleed, chrome winking off its fender, grill, running boards. Standing high in the late-afternoon light. It was massive, imposing, sexy—if a pickup could be sexy. I was pretty certain this one had decided it was. As I glided past, I couldn't see through its dark-tinted windows. It was probably just as done up inside. It sat squarely in the middle of the key, commanding the court.

Mr. Kenshaw turned off his mower and stopped cutting the strip of grass between our houses.

"Quite the truck," he said with a low whistle.

I nodded. I knew he wasn't just cutting the grass but was also spying on us. I almost told him to mind his own business but decided I didn't need to get into trouble.

Opening up the garage, I let my bike fall as I went into the house and kicked off my shoes.

"Jordan?" I heard my dad calling. "Is that you?"

Junior nearly slid past me as he darted down the hall and tried to stop. "It's Jay, Mr. R."

"What are you doing here?" I asked both of them.

"You weren't answering my texts," my dad said.

"Or mine either," Junior added. "I came back to look for you."

"We were worried." My dad was in the Bulls jersey and basketball shorts my mom and I had ordered for his birthday. A brace hugged his bad right knee.

I yanked my phone out of my pocket and saw a lot more notices for texts, missed calls and voice mails than before. A lot more.

"Wow," I said. "You two didn't need to blow up my phone."

My dad crossed his arms over his chest. "I was worried because I didn't know where you were."

"I think since you don't live here, there's lots of things you won't know about," I replied.

"This is still my house."

"But you don't actually live here anymore." I turned to Junior and pointed. "Neither do you."

Junior looked surprised and hurt. I felt bad. He pursed his lips and nodded. "I'll get going then."

"I know you're angry at me, but Junior doesn't deserve that," my dad said. He gave Junior's shoulder a squeeze.

Junior smiled at him for a second before slipping his shoes on and walking past me.

I turned as Junior stepped down into the garage. "Wait," I said. "I didn't mean...I'm..."

"Dude, that was just rude. Settle down and you can call me later," Junior said. "My mom is expecting me home for dinner. Sorry for being worried about you. I'll try not to do that again."

Junior shoved his hands in his pockets as he walked away, stopping for a minute to gaze up at the truck.

My dad moved to my side. "You should patch things up with him. You two are like brothers, like family."

"I'm learning that family doesn't always mean as much as I thought."

My father looked hurt. I wasn't sorry for hurting him. In fact, I was going to double down on it. "And he's not your son. You barely have time for the one you have. Don't go getting Junior to check in on me."

"I'm sorry I haven't been around, but work has exploded. I've been working like mad at the plant and handing out pink slips, with all the faulty parts deliberately rolling off the line. Besides, it's not like I've been the one ignoring you."

I looked at his clothing. "It looks like you still found time to shoot some hoops."

"A friend offered to come by, so we played a little to help me decompress."

"Is that who owns the truck?"

"Yes, he's sitting in the truck right now, waiting for me."

My dad's phone rang. He pulled it out of his pocket. "I, uh…" he said. "Jordan, I need to go out to the driveway for a minute."

I followed him outside.

My mom was standing beside the red truck. Hers was parked on the road. The driver's door of the truck opened. A mountain emerged into the sunlight. A man who stood taller than my father walked in front of the truck. The guy's T-shirt stretched over his wide chest and gut, hair blooming from the neck of it and almost joining his bushy red beard. His head was shaved at the sides.

"What's going on?" Mom asked, looking from the mountain to my dad. "Who is this?"

"This is, um, we're..." my dad stammered, looking between my mom, the man and me.

"Sorry for blocking the driveway. Chris was worried and insisted we head over when he couldn't get hold of your son," the man said in a deep voice.

"And who is he?" Mom asked Dad.

The giant extended his hand and swallowed my mom's in it as they shook. "Apologies. I'm Brodie Greaves."

My mother stared down the giant gripping her hand.

"I'm...we're—" He stopped, looked from my mom to my dad and then back. "Um, friends."

"Friends?" my mother asked, raising an eyebrow.

My dad cut in. "We're, well...friends."

My mother took back her hand. "Don't you think it's a little too soon to bring your boyfriend here?"

Boyfriend. This was my dad's *boyfriend.* This supersized man certainly was no boy. Neither was my dad.

"I didn't mean to upset anyone," Brodie said.

My mom burst into tears and fled toward the house.

I stood there, stunned, watching her leave.

"I better go and check on her," my dad said.

"Don't," I said. "I think you've already done enough."

I turned and went back into the house. My father called out, but I didn't turn around. My mom needed me, and I needed to be with her.

Mom returned to the kitchen. She had been gone for over twenty minutes, saying she needed time before we talked.

"I just got off the phone with your father," she said as she sat down.

"How was that?"

"Not great. I suggested he call me before coming over from now on." She paused. "Especially if he's planning on bringing along 'guests.'"

Is that what we were calling him? If he was a guest, I figured we weren't saying the 'unwelcome' part out loud.

She continued, "He shouldn't have done that. He shouldn't have sprung that on either of us. But he's not the only one who needs to call or text to let me know where he is."

"But I didn't—" I began. "Sorry."

"You're not in trouble," she said, "but I need to know where you are when you change plans. We're all figuring out how this is going to work."

"Yeah, okay. Sorry, Mom. Hey, I made something for us."

I pulled four grilled cheese sandwiches out of the oven, where I'd put them to keep them warm.

"I thought I smelled something."

I put them on two plates. We sat and ate quietly.

Finally my mom broke the silence. "I made a fool out of myself. I do that around your father it seems."

"I didn't think it was that bad."

My mom laughed. "You're a terrible liar. One day, when you have a wife..." She trailed off, and her eyes got glassy. "I shouldn't assume."

"I'm not gay," I shot out.

"I wasn't saying that!" my mom protested. "I meant I shouldn't assume you'd ever want to be married after the mess your own parents are."

I thought about Tammy. I liked her for sure. Marriage? So far all we'd done was kiss. Twice.

"Did you always want to be married?" I asked.

"God no, but then I got to know your dad."

Mom took another bite of her grilled cheese. "He had something about him. Maybe it was that he was so quiet, and I read that as being the strong, silent type. I always felt like he'd take care of whatever happened, and I was good at letting him be the strong one. Actually, we were both with other people when we met. Your dad used to get teased about his secret girlfriend no one had ever seen." Mom wrinkled her brow. "I wonder..."

She let the sentence evaporate, and we both let the thought sit between us. Eventually Mom picked up her sandwich again.

"You're going to call Junior tonight. Right?"

As much as I didn't want to take the first step, I knew I was the one who had to go first if I was going to fix things between us. It was my fault. I'd been the jerk. "I guess."

"Before you go…your dad wants to pick you up tomorrow. You don't have to go with him, but I really think you should."

"I don't want to."

"I know, but you both might need to. At least think about it. If you still want some space in the morning, I'll back you up. Now, how about I clear the dishes and you call Junior."

I went up to my room. I stared at my phone before hitting his number from my favorites list.

I waited three rings before he picked up and said, "You don't need to say it. I forgive you."

"I didn't say anything," I answered.

"Because you don't need to. I just said that."

We were both quiet for a minute.

"You should ease up on your dad," Junior said. "Anyone can see he's been trying really hard."

"It's not that simple."

"Why not?" Junior asked. "Where were you earlier anyway?"

I felt my cheeks burn a little. "I rode over to Ridge Town."

"To see Tammy?"

"Well, it wasn't to see Aaron."

"I want to hear everything. But first, where did your dad get that awesome new truck?"

I rolled my eyes. It *was* a beautiful vehicle. "It's his boyfriend's. He was sitting inside it. I met him. Me and Mom."

"Okay, that's a shocker."

"Welcome to the club."

"What's he like?"

"It's not like we talked much, but he's even bigger than my father."

"Whoa. That is big."

"Look, I don't really want to talk about this, about him."

"Good, because I'd really rather hear more about your going to see Tammy. Did it involve any more kissing?"

"Maybe. A little."

"I want to hear everything."

"She is pretty cool."

"She must have been pretty supportive and stuff when you told her. About your father, I mean."

"Yeah, she is. Her parents separated. She knows about him moving out."

"That's not what I mean, and you know it. Tammy has all sorts of rainbow buttons on her bag. She was cool, right?"

Of course, I knew exactly what he meant.

I didn't respond.

Junior broke the silence. "You didn't tell her."

"It didn't come up."

"It wouldn't come up unless you mentioned it. Why didn't you?"

"I don't know. I just didn't. Seeing her again, going up to her house like that, was already embarrassing enough without making it worse."

"Why would it be worse?"

"Look, you wouldn't understand because you don't have a—" I stopped myself.

Junior was silent for a minute. "Were you going to say 'a father'? Just because my dad is dead doesn't mean I can't understand."

"I didn't say that."

"Then what were you going to say?"

On the edge of arguing with Junior again, I wasn't sure I even knew what I was going to say. It was a fact that Junior didn't have a father. He also didn't have a girlfriend or parents who had split up. It was so hard to put in words, but I had to try. "What I'm going through isn't what you've gone through. Your dad didn't choose to die."

"And you think your father *chose* to be gay?"

"He chose how he's acting," I said.

"If people got to choose," Junior continued, as if I hadn't said anything, "don't you think they'd choose something easier? Something that can't hurt them?"

"The last two days have been hard. I don't want to fight with you anymore."

"Don't you ever think it's hard on your dad too?"

I didn't know how to answer that.

"He had his new boyfriend drive into the middle of something hard to make sure you were okay, Jordan," Junior said.

He'd called me Jordan. He never called me Jordan.

"Everyone in the neighborhood probably saw that truck. It didn't exactly blend in. He risked whatever is going on just to know you were safe."

Brodie didn't exactly blend in either, no more than his truck did. And Mr. Kenshaw had probably watched everything.

When I didn't respond, Junior said, "I don't really want to fight with you either. You might want to tell Tammy soon. Secrets don't keep long in this town."

"My father doesn't live in this town anymore."

"That doesn't matter. You should tell her," Junior said. "She's going to hear about it. Peeps will be talking about it."

My stomach decided to tie itself into a lump. Of course people were going to talk. They already were. I could guess what they were going to say about my father. What were they going to say about us? About me?

"I gotta go," I said. "I'll see you Monday."

"Wait, Jay. There's something I want to say."

"Can't it wait? I've had enough heavy stuff for one day."

"But I—" Junior began. "Sure, it can wait. See you Monday."

"Sure. Monday." I ended the call and quickly turned off the phone. I didn't want to talk to Junior anymore that night. I didn't want to talk to anybody.

Eighteen

Mom was a different type of driver than my dad. She didn't run stop signs or sit on other cars' bumpers. She rarely even honked. But she stepped on the gas and took off pretty fast from a stop, and sometimes she mumbled under her breath at other drivers. I often wondered what she would do with the Camaro, but my father never let anybody else drive it.

"It's been a relief," she said as she drove me to school on Monday, "not working in Franklin. I can go in and do my job and just be Amanda. Nobody except my closest friends know anything, and even they don't know everything."

I understood what she meant by everything. Yesterday I had texted my dad and told him I didn't want to hang out yet. I'd spent most of the day shooting hoops and texting Tammy. A lot of the texts were smiley faces and LOLs. There wasn't a good time to slip in anything about my dad. I waited between replies to Junior and sent him mainly one-word responses when he texted me in the afternoon. As a churchgoer, Junior had to know Sundays were supposed to be a day of rest, and I needed a break.

We pulled up to the school. "Have a good day," said Mom. She leaned across the cab of her truck and kissed me on the cheek before I had a chance to stop her. She reached into the back seat. "I made you lunch. It's nothing fancy. Plain old ham and cheese."

I took the brown paper bag. "Thanks. See you tonight." I slipped out of the car, thinking that plain old nothing fancy wasn't so terrible sometimes.

Tammy wasn't anywhere I looked before class. I wasn't sure what I was going to tell her or how, if I even worked up the nerve. Junior was right. Secrets didn't keep, especially ones that were juicy and ripe.

Minutes before homeroom, I went to my locker.

"Hey, J.R.," a girl named Angelique said. She leaned against the locker beside me.

"Hey," I answered.

"The girls' basketball team tryouts have started, and I'm going out for captain," she said. "Maybe you'd be willing to show me a few techniques sometime. Help me the way you helped Tammy."

"Sure. I guess. Sometime."

"What are you doing after practice today?"

"Heading home probably."

"You could come over to my place if you're free. We've got a hoop on the driveway."

My mouth went dry. "We can play ball, but, uh, I'm probably going to go over to Tammy's place."

Angelique laughed. Nothing was even remotely funny.

"Maybe tomorrow. Considering everything," she said, "it might be nice to hang out with a girl that's less *Tammy*."

"What?"

"Like, why does she think she's too good to be on the girls' team? What is she trying to prove?" Angelique smoothed her ponytail over her shoulder. "Why can't she just be a regular girl?"

I didn't answer.

Angelique giggled. "Think about it. Tomorrow is good if you haven't got anything planned." She tossed her hair and walked past me into homeroom.

Throughout morning classes, I kept thinking more whispers and notes than usual were going around when teachers' backs were turned. Whenever I turned my head to check, I heard giggles or snickers. I tried to tell myself they weren't directed at me, but I kept having that weird sensation that people were staring at me.

Walking the halls between classes, the feeling remained. No one had said anything, but that only made me more suspicious that people were talking. I knew if I asked Junior, he'd tell me things weren't all about me. Even if they were all about my dad, I was still the one who had to deal with them.

I grabbed my lunch out of my locker. A soccer player named Noah jogged past me, and we bumped shoulders. He shot me a dirty look.

"Watch it," I mumbled, more to myself than to him.

"You watch it."

"Seriously?" I asked, turning around to face him.

"You want some type of special treatment, Ryker? You may think you own the courts, but you don't own the halls. Watch where you're going."

I balled my fists but just shook my head.

Noah rolled his eyes and turned to talk to two of his soccer friends.

I was going to go have lunch, but I heard Noah say, "I know. So gay."

I jumped into his face. "Did you want to say something?"

"Whatever."

"What did you say?" I demanded.

"I wasn't talking to you."

"Then who were you talking to?"

Noah rolled his eyes again. "You're acting like your little girlfriend and getting worked up over nothing."

Without stopping to think, I shoved him with both hands and knocked him back a couple of steps. "Don't talk about Tammy, and don't talk about my family!"

Noah recovered his balance and came forward. "Who said anything about your family? You need to back off."

"You back off."

He rolled his eyes one more time. I dropped my lunch bag, grabbed him by the shoulders and pushed him hard. He stumbled back into his friends. If they hadn't caught him, he would have gone down. I gritted my teeth. Noah bent his knees and charged at me, aiming at my middle. I only had enough time to reach over his back and hook my arms under his armpits. We struggled back and forth and then broke apart. I hooked his arm and spun him to the ground. He instantly bounced back to his feet.

A crowd gathered around us and began to chant, "Fight! Fight! Fight!" We moved back and forth like dancers. The crowd closed in, pushing the two of us closer together.

A hand grabbed me by the shoulder. I turned, ready to strike out.

"Who started this?" Mr. Tanner asked the crowd. People at the edges started to drift away. He kept his hand on my shoulder. "Anyone care to answer?"

"Ryker pushed him first," one of Noah's friends said.

"Jordan?" Mr. Tanner asked.

I looked away and shrugged. I had pushed him first.

"Both of you to the office."

"But it was nothing!" Noah said. "We were just, uh, fooling around."

He had a pleading, go-along-with-it expression. I was still angry at him, but it was better if we could get out of this. I didn't want a suspension.

"Yeah, just goofing around," I said. "You know, soccer guys think they're better than basketball guys, and we know that's not true."

Mr. Tanner looked skeptical, but I was hoping he wanted to believe us. "Okay, everybody, the show is over. All of you, get to lunch!"

Everybody started away quickly, including Noah, leaving me standing there with Mr. Tanner.

"Jordan, pick up your bag and come with me. We're going to the office."

"But we were just fooling around. Why do I have to go to the office?" I demanded.

"I was looking for you before all of this. Come with me. Now."

"Sir—" I began.

Mr. Tanner nodded at my now ripped paper bag with the sandwich my mom had made in it. I picked it up. We walked side by side to the principal's office. Mr. Tanner told me to sit and eat while he went inside. I didn't touch my sandwich.

Mr. Tanner asked me into the office not too much later.

Ms. Jones sat behind her desk. Mr. Tanner and a woman I'd never met before were standing. Was she a supply teacher, and if so, why was she here?

"Please, sit down, Jordan," Ms. Jones said. "Mr. Tanner told us you were involved in some sort of scuffle."

"I guess, but it was nothing."

"Care to tell us about it?" Ms. Jones asked.

"Not really. It wasn't anything. Noah sort of bumped into me and then said some stuff."

"They told me they were just fooling around," Mr. Tanner said. "But if I hadn't come along, it could have become a full-out fight."

The other woman nodded before she sat down in the chair beside me, shifting it so she was facing me.

"Oh, I'm sorry, I probably should introduce myself. I'm Mrs. Mercer."

"I was coming to get you so you could meet Mrs. Mercer," Mr. Tanner explained.

"I'm the school social worker. I was asked to come in and see you. I'm curious. The comments that started things today. Did they have anything to do with your father?"

For the first time, I really looked at Mrs. Mercer, with her floral blouse, delicately framed glasses and hair threaded with white strands. What did she know about my dad? What did they all know?

"Your mother and I spoke this morning," she said.

"My mom went to work."

"She phoned me first thing this morning," Ms. Jones said. "She wanted the school to be aware of your situation."

Was that what we were calling it, a situation? It had nothing to do with school, so why had my mom called?

"After your mother and I spoke, I involved Mrs. Mercer and had her call your mother," Ms. Jones added.

"We're all concerned, especially after the incident just now, about how you're processing things," Mrs. Mercer explained. "Is there anything you'd like to share?"

I didn't answer. Instead I stared at Mrs. Mercer's hands. She wasn't wearing a wedding band.

"Jordan, you need to talk to her," Mr. Tanner said. "I can't have someone on my team fighting in the halls."

"Or fighting anywhere," Ms. Jones added. "After talking together, we've agreed you will be seeing Mrs. Mercer for a while to make sure you're adjusting as well as you can. She's here to help."

"I don't need help."

"We all need help," Mrs. Mercer said.

"This is not optional, Jordan. You'll have to attend sessions with Mrs. Mercer. I'll be speaking to your father when he gets here. Your parents have arranged for him to pick you up."

"Do you mean pick me up after practice?" I asked.

"We've already called him to come get you."

"I'm being suspended?" I exclaimed.

"Not suspended. Just taking an afternoon off to get some perspective."

I was speechless.

"And I'll set up a schedule for our talks." Mrs. Mercer kept leaning in and holding the arm of my chair.

I slouched. I didn't want counseling. My dad had quit when he didn't want any more of it. But I was stuck. They could force me to have sessions with Mrs. Mercer. They could make me sit in the same room. But I'd stick to my guns. They couldn't force me to talk.

Nineteen

I sat on a bench outside the office. I hadn't been happy to begin with but was even more upset when they told me it was my dad who was coming to get me. Dad didn't say anything to me when he came in. He was ushered into the office with Mrs. Mercer and Ms. Jones. Mr. Tanner had gone to teach his afternoon classes.

I looked up and saw Tammy, her backpack of buttons clinking. She dropped it as she sat down beside me, sliding her hand on top of mine.

"I heard you got into trouble for fighting with Noah," she said.

"It really wasn't much of a fight."

"Good, because I'm not into violence."

"Not now."

"Let me finish," Tammy said. "I know you haven't been yourself today. Junior told me about your dad. Why didn't you tell me what was going on?"

I wanted to move away from her but kept still. "What was I supposed to say?"

"I'd have understood. I *do* understand."

But did she? I mean, Junior was right that Tammy was cool in a progressive-thinking way. She'd understand all about my dad. But would she understand how I wasn't exactly happy with everything going on at home and with him? Or would she get on her soapbox and tell me how great and brave my father was and that it was never too late to be true to yourself and what I should be doing for him? I didn't want to hear any of it.

I shifted slightly away from her on the bench. "I knew you would," I said. "But this is my play to call, Tammy. I need to figure it out on my own. Can you let me do that?"

Tammy chewed her lip but nodded. "Sure. I'm here though. You know that. Right?"

"I know. But actually, why are you here in the office and not in class?"

"I was sent to see Ms. Jones."

"What did you do wrong?"

Tammy smiled and pulled a file folder out of her backpack. "I'm actually trying to do something right. Let's see," she said as she flipped through pages. "Here! Unsustainable palm oil in cafeteria foods. Do you know how damaging palm farms can be? It's not only the deforestation."

"And those other papers?" I asked.

"I keep a folder of ways this school can become a leader and take a stance on issues."

"And you believe in all these?"

"Of course," she said. "But I wanted to come to the office to talk to you, so I asked if I could discuss them with Ms. Jones."

"You used a global issue to come see how I was doing?"

"Don't flatter yourself too much. It really is serious."

I leaned in, cupped her cheek in my hand, then kissed her.

She pushed me away gently. "Not here," she whispered.

Ms. Jones's door opened. My dad stepped out.

"Do you have your things?" he asked.

I nodded.

Tammy stood up. "Mr. Ryker," she said. "Nice to see you again."

"How are you, Tammy?"

"Pretty good. I came to talk to Ms. Jones about sustainable palm oil."

My dad raised an eyebrow. "I'll need to hear about it another time. Jordan, we need to get going."

I stood, and my dad placed a hand behind my neck as we walked out of the building. As soon as we hit the parking lot, I shrugged it off and hurried to the passenger side of the Camaro.

"Do you want to talk about it?" he asked as he started the car and did his checks.

"No."

Then he surprised me by saying, "Me either." He backed out of the parking spot and put on his signals to turn out of the lot.

"Do you want to put on the radio?"

"Not really."

"Do you want to play some ball before my night shift?"

"No."

"Did what happened today have anything to do with our situation?" my dad asked.

"Our situation or your situation?" I snapped.

"Okay, my situation."

"Yeah, it did."

"I'm sorry. I wish I could say I'm surprised. I've had things said to me too."

"What did you expect?" I demanded.

"I'm not sure. I guess I expected better from some people."

Did he mean me?

"People I've known for years, that I thought were my friends, are treating me differently." He paused. "Are you sure you don't want to talk about it?"

"I don't want to talk to anybody about anything."

"We don't have to talk, but I need to get something to eat, and I've got some groceries to pick up."

My dad drove below the speed limit. We passed the town sign and kept going, turning in the opposite direction from the town where he now lived. I lost track of where we were going.

He pulled up to the curb in a grungy-looking area. The buildings all looked like industrial spaces that had been boarded up decades ago. Now there was one of those fancy coffee bars on one corner and a knitting store beside it. We stopped in front of a butcher shop.

"Let's go," my dad said as he opened his door.

I entered the store after him. The space behind the counter was filled with the shine of knives stuck to the walls. This was fancy. Since when did my dad shop here? Then I heard an unmistakable deep voice. Brodie. Why had my dad brought me here? I almost turned and walked away. Was he trying to make a bad day even worse?

Brodie was talking to a woman on our side of the counter. "We'll have venison in a few weeks if the season is good. Last year we saw plenty of deer, but it was better for the populations to let them be. I've got that roast in the back. I'll wrap it for you." Everything in the place was immaculate, all stainless steel and polished wood—except for Brodie, who was wearing an apron smeared with red-brown streaks.

Brodie nodded at my dad as he moved behind the counter and silently slid over two packages wrapped in butcher paper and tied with twine. My dad picked them up and headed to a table by the window.

Dad pushed one of the packages at me as we sat. "Don't worry," he said. "It's not anything weird. Brodie's barbecue is to die for."

Dad had never described anything as 'to die for.' I rolled my eyes but unwrapped the package. It smelled good, and I was hungry. I took a big bite, and the beef or whatever was inside fell apart before I could chew it.

The customer left. Brodie washed his hands and snapped on his black leather cuffs before he came over.

"Jordan, Chris," he said. "How're those sandwiches?"

"Great," my dad said. "If you can't tell by how far through his Jordan is."

"How's the bread? I switched suppliers. I want to support someone local, but I'm not sure, and the delivery has been spotty. What do you think about the taste, Jordan?"

"It's fine."

"It doesn't hold up," my dad said. "You need something a bit more toothsome."

"Like, crunchier?"

My dad took another bite and chewed. "Maybe not so spongy. It's too light, too airy."

I finished eating. "I thought we were getting groceries."

The shop's phone rang. Brodie went behind the counter to answer it. He ripped off a piece of butcher paper from a big roll on the wall and wrote an order on it.

More than once my dad glanced over at Brodie, who winked back at him. My dad got a big, dumb smile on his face.

I huffed as I leaned back in the chair, wondering if I could ask to sit in the car until they were done. I'd thought I wasn't in trouble for fighting earlier. I was wrong. My dad had invented this bizarre form of mental torture by forcing me to sit and watch him flirt with his new boyfriend.

"Everything's ready, Chris," Brodie said as he hung up the phone. "It's vacuum-sealed and divided up for you and Amanda."

It bugged me to hear this guy mention my mother's name and not even get it right. Really, nobody ever called her Amanda.

"What do I owe you?" my dad asked, standing up and reaching for his wallet.

"We'll settle up later," Brodie replied as he began placing bags on the counter. "You need help getting to the car?"

"We're good," Dad said. "I'll have the money for you next time I see you. Don't forget to add in the sandwiches."

"They're on the house. It's Jordan's first time here. I'll see you later in the week, Chris. Good to see you, Jordan."

"Sure," I said as Dad handed me some bags to carry.

We put them into the trunk of the car and then got in.

Once we were driving again, I asked, "Did we have to do that?"

"I wasn't planning on having to come and get you this afternoon. This was already planned."

"Why couldn't you just buy stuff from the meat department at the local grocery store or have Mom bring it back from her work?"

"Brodie insisted on stocking us up at cost. It would have made no sense and been insulting if I had turned him down. Even your mom agreed. He sells local, organic goods that are responsibly sourced. I thought hanging around with Tammy, you'd appreciate that. We're saving a lot of money because of him."

"So he's treating you like a charity case?" I asked.

"No," my dad said. He stopped at a red light. "No. Jordan, I think you'd like Brodie. If you gave him a chance. He's a good man."

I kept looking out the window. Brodie might be the best guy ever, but he wasn't getting any chance from me or anything else.

Twenty

I looked at the big clock at the end of the gym. This morning's practice had less than twenty minutes to go before we'd get changed and ready for classes. It hadn't been a good one. Some players—those sitting at the end of the bench during games—weren't taking this seriously enough. That bothered me, and as the captain I had an obligation to let them know. Junior had quietly advised me to "slow my roll."

He was right about that. It had been a long, hard week. The basketball court was the place I felt least annoyed and most at home. It was all familiar—being on the court, running plays, shooting hoops. Nothing had changed. The team was perfect, 8 and 0. I was playing well. I was captain— at least, co-captain—even if I was being "watched" by the office.

I tried to slow my roll, but a lot of things irritated me. Junior had told me I was being "snippety," his way of saying I was snapping at people. I wanted to believe it was just

Junior being oversensitive because he liked to get along with everybody, but both my mom and Tammy had said similar things to me this week already.

"Okay, lots of work to be done!" Coach yelled. "Let's try the high pick and roll between Junior and Aaron. Once Tammy inbounds the ball, I want Jordan underneath, opposite side, drawing defensive coverage as an alternative threat and to pick up any rebounds."

"Coach, it's me shooting. Do you actually think there's going to be a rebound?" Junior blew on his knuckles and polished them on his shirt.

Everybody laughed.

"I like the confidence," Coach said. "But remember, there's a fine line between confidence and delusion."

More laughter, but this time at Junior. He gasped and held his hands to his chest as if he'd been shot with an arrow. He never minded stuff like this.

Junior gave me a look and a little nod. I knew what he meant. Coach was becoming an actual coach. The practice hadn't gone well, but it wasn't because of Coach Tanner. He was starting to get this stuff. He was sounding like a coach, even calling out some plays during the game.

Tammy took the ball and got ready to pass. I noticed Donavan playing off of Junior because he knew what the play was going to be and he didn't have to cover him for the shot.

"Donavan, quit cheating!" I yelled. "Play it straight up! Go out on him or get off the court!"

Donavan shot me a look, then moved a half step closer. Practice like you play, Junior and I always said. Donavan was still cheating, which meant he was cheating all of us.

Tammy was playing in this practice with the rest of the starters. She was getting more time, and Coach trusted her on throw-ins. Her basketball IQ was getting higher all the time. She was smart, and she learned quickly. She faked a pass to Jing in the corner, then hit Junior as he curled above the top of the key. Aaron set up at the top of the key, and I slid down low on the block on the other side. As the ball went to Aaron, Junior flashed by and took it. I noticed Donavan cheat again and decided to call my own audible. He wasn't the only person who knew what was coming up next.

I quickly came forward. I planted my feet and set a pick. He was going to have to go through me to cover his man. Junior curved around the corner. As he brushed by me, Donavan turned to follow him. I was right there. He crashed into me, head down, face first, bouncing off my chest, falling backward and landing with a thud. He screamed out in pain and grabbed at his nose—which didn't stop the blood from gushing down his chin.

Everybody stopped. Donavan screamed again, and everyone unfroze. Two of the guys dropped to their knees beside him as Coach ran to the bench, grabbed a towel and rushed back.

"Let me have a look!" Coach exclaimed. He was trying to sound calm.

Junior came to my side as everybody else clustered around Donavan. He took me by the arm and pulled me aside.

"Hard pick for a practice," he whispered.

"Practice like you play."

"You should tell him you're sorry and didn't mean to hurt him."

"It wouldn't have happened if he hadn't cheated."

"Harsh, man. You know the right thing to do, unless you really did want to hurt him."

"Of course I didn't." At least, not hurt him this bad. I walked over. "Sorry, man. I was just setting a pick."

"It's okay," said Donavan after a moment. "I should have had my head up."

I almost answered, Yes, you should have, and you shouldn't have been cheating to start with—but instead I nodded and said sorry again and "I didn't mean to hurt you," like Junior had advised. That was the truth, and it was also a lie. I had meant to stick him good, but I hadn't meant to make him bleed.

Coach helped Donavan to his feet. Everybody gave him a little clap in support. I clapped too.

"Everybody, do five laps and then shoot around," Coach Tanner said as he walked Donavan to the bench.

"Grab a ball!" I called. "Let's dribble while we do laps."

Everybody took a ball out of the bin and started to move. Tammy fell in beside me.

"Do you think his nose is broken?" she asked.

"I couldn't really see."

"If it is, you might end up starting," Aaron said to Tammy. He was right behind us.

"I'm worried about my teammate, not about being one of the starters. Stop being a jerk."

"Me? A jerk? It was your boyfriend who planted the pick."

Was he calling me a jerk? I turned my head. I was going to say something, but before I could, Aaron continued.

"Not that I'm blaming J.R. You told him to stop cheating, and he didn't. What is it that you and Junior keep yapping about? Practice like you play?" Aaron said.

"Nice, Aaron, really supportive of your teammate," Tammy replied.

"I am supporting one of my teammates. My co-captain. Besides, did you hear him scream? Like a little girl."

Tammy narrowed her eyes at her brother but kept quiet.

We kept dribbling until we finished our laps. Some of the players weren't running any harder than they'd been practicing, but I didn't think I could say anything more.

The three of us, Aaron, Tammy and I, went down under the far hoop and started shooting. Junior joined us.

"You know, Tammy, I thought you'd have figured out by now that this is the boys' basketball team. Not the girls' or ballroom dancing," Aaron said.

"Because those things are *so* similar," Tammy replied.

"Ballroom dancing is pretty tough," Junior said as he threw up a shot. "I took it for three years when I was little." He chased down the rebound.

"He's kidding, right?" Tammy asked.

"He's not," I said. I'd taken up a spot on the low block to practice turnaround fakes. "Their church was offering free classes for boys, so his mom made him go. Ballroom boys are rare."

"My mother might have made me, but I didn't mind," Junior said. "Even at eight I thought it was pretty cool to put my arms around my partner. Her name was Rosita and—" Junior changed his posture and lifted his body into position, one hand poised in midair and the other extended. "Rosita was—"

"Extremely beautiful," I finished his sentence.

"She *was*. And an older woman. I think she was eleven. I wonder where she is now."

"You're speaking about her like she's some type of object," Tammy said.

"If you do the math, she's probably almost seventeen by now," I commented.

"Now you're trying to distract me!" Junior replied as he started to fan himself. "That Rosita is probably the most beautiful woman in the world. I can picture her, late at night, crying into her pillow and praying that someday her Junior will return."

I couldn't help but laugh as Junior stepped and turned as if dancing.

"Junior!" Junior called out, almost trilling like a songbird in his falsetto. "I miss yooooou! Please, all that is good in the world, bring back my Junior!"

"If you miss it that much, maybe you should sign up again," I suggested.

"Maybe you should go with him," Aaron said.

"Why would I want to do that?"

"Because, you know, the fruit doesn't fall far from the tree. You and Junior could be partners, like in everything else."

"What are you talking about?"

He laughed. "I'm talking about how you and Junior are almost attached. Follow in the footsteps of your dad, maybe? He found a guy to lead him around the dance floor. Didn't he?" He laughed again.

"Shut up, Aaron!" Tammy exclaimed.

"What, can't your boyfriend take a little joke?"

"That's not a joke," Tammy said.

"Didn't your dad used to play basketball too?" Aaron asked me.

"He went through college on a scholarship," Junior said.

"Makes you wonder if you're the only member of your family who dated one of his teammates." Aaron started laughing again. "They say history repeats itself."

I rushed at Aaron. Junior got between us, holding me back. I struggled against Junior.

"You can't afford to be in another fight—they'll suspend you," Junior said.

I still tried to get to Aaron.

"The team needs you. He's not worth it."

I stopped fighting to get free, but Junior kept holding on to me.

"Maybe we should talk to Coach about a third change room. One for the girls, one for the guys and one for Jordan." Aaron bent his wrist high above his head as if shooting a foul. "Then you wouldn't need to worry about controlling yourself around us boys. Like father, like son."

Junior released his grip, spun around and planted a punch right in Aaron's face. Aaron went down even harder than Donavan had!

"Before I start calling parents, somebody needs to explain what happened. Who's going to start?" Ms. Jones asked.

Nobody volunteered.

We sat in her office, in two groups—Junior, me and Tammy on one side of the room, Aaron on the other, with Coach Tanner beside him. Aaron held a clump of wet paper towels to his nose. It was still bleeding, but it wasn't broken. Luckily, neither was Donavan's.

"Okay, as I understand it, Junior, you punched Aaron. Is that correct?"

"Yes, ma'am."

Before he could say anything more, Tammy jumped in. "He only punched my brother because he got there before I had a chance to punch him. My brother is the one who should be in serious trouble."

"Are you saying that he hit Junior first?" Ms. Jones asked.

Ms. Jones turned to Mr. Tanner. He raised his hands

and shrugged. "I was too busy dealing with Donavan's bleeding nose. I didn't see what happened."

"Did Junior punch Donavan as well?" she asked.

"No, that was me," I said, looking at Junior.

"You punched Donavan?"

"No, he ran into me. It was a pick, a basketball play. It was an accident." That was only half-true.

"But it's my brother who needs to be reprimanded," Tammy said.

"Shut up, Tammy!" Aaron snapped. His voice was muffled because he was still holding his nose.

"We will not be having that sort of language in here," Ms. Jones warned. She turned to Tammy. "Why do you believe your brother should be reprimanded?"

"He said homophobic things. He's part of the problem at this school."

Ms. Jones raised her eyebrows at Tammy.

"Ma'am," Tammy added quickly.

Aaron pulled the paper towel away. His nosebleed had mostly stopped. "I was joking around. Get a sense of humor."

"It isn't funny," Tammy said.

"Can't anybody take a joke anymore?" Aaron asked.

"Nobody was laughing," Junior said.

"Junior tried to stop me from taking a swing at Aaron," I said. I knew I could land in more trouble after the scuffle on Monday, but I couldn't let Junior go down by himself.

"So he stopped you and decided to do it himself?"

"Well...yeah," Junior admitted.

Ms. Jones let out a long sigh. "So let me get this straight. Jordan accidently hurt Donavan. Aaron said some inappropriate things that he felt were jokes, but they weren't funny, only hurtful. Junior, who was originally holding Jordan back from attacking Aaron, punched Aaron in the face. And Tammy would have punched her brother, but Junior did it first. Is that it?"

We all nodded.

"Tammy, you're free to go. You didn't actually do anything."

"But I really feel—" Tammy began.

"Not now, Tammy. Take Jordan with you," she said. "Even though he was angry, he didn't actually strike anybody."

"Only because Junior stopped him," Aaron said. "He was ready to hit me."

"But he didn't," Ms. Jones replied.

"What about me?" Aaron asked.

"You'll be receiving a detention and a counseling session, or two, from Mrs. Mercer. I'd like you to explain why you think your jokes are funny. Do you have any objection to that?"

He shook his head.

"Then you can go too. That leaves Junior," she said. "I understand your motivation. You felt provoked and were protecting your friend."

"There's a *but* coming, isn't there?" Junior asked.

"But you struck another student. I have no choice but to give you a one-day suspension."

"That's not fair!" I protested. "It should be me getting suspended, not Junior."

"Quiet, Jay," Junior said.

"I can't have my students fighting. This is twice in one week that members of the basketball team got into physical altercations. I feel I need to send you a message about fighting during school hours."

"When does my suspension start?" Junior asked.

"Today. You'll serve a one-day in-house suspension."

"I understand," Junior said. "Does that mean at the end of the day it's over?"

"Of course. We're not keeping you overnight."

"Great. Then I'll be able to play in tonight's game."

Ms. Jones shook her head. "Your one-day suspension includes classes and all school and extracurricular activities for the day, including field trips and team sports."

"I can't play tonight?"

"That seems a little rough," Mr. Tanner said.

Ms. Jones raised her eyebrows at him.

"But I have to agree with the decision," Mr. Tanner added.

"Fine. You three go to class. Junior, you're to remain in my office."

Tammy, Aaron and I got to our feet. Part of me wanted to leave as quickly as I could. The other part wanted to stay with Junior, but there was no point.

We walked out and closed the door behind us. We'd gone no more than a dozen steps when Aaron spun around to block my way.

"Step aside," Tammy said.

"Or what?" Aaron asked. "Your boyfriend can't lay a hand

on me or he'll get suspended and be out of the game too."

So fast I almost missed it, Tammy slapped Aaron across the face. "He can't, but I can," she said.

Aaron's nose began to bleed again. He pressed the wad of paper towel to it.

"I'm your brother! And you don't even believe in violence. Do you really want to be suspended too?"

Tammy shrugged. "Go in there and tell them your baby sister slapped the stupid off your face. Or hit me back. I dare you."

"You know I'd never hit a girl."

"You better never hit her," I warned.

Aaron glowered over the paper towel. "This isn't over."

"You got that right," I said.

I held up three fingers. He looked confused. Tammy held my other hand.

"What does that mean?" he demanded.

"We have three games to go until we walk away with the trophy. Now get out of my face."

He hesitated before holding up three fingers himself. He nodded. "I can wait."

Twenty-One

I waved up into the stands. Junior and Donavan waved back. Junior had been allowed to come as a spectator. Donavan had to sit out as a precaution in case he had a concussion. In different ways, I was responsible for both of them having to sit out.

One row behind them was Ms. Jones. As far as I knew, she had never been to a basketball game this year or the year before. She wasn't here to watch basketball so much as to watch me. I understood why. I figured that Mrs. Mercer would be getting a full report.

"You ready?" Coach asked.

"Sure."

"Not the confident answer I was hoping for. Either way, win or lose, we're in the playoffs."

"If we win, we get a bye in the first round and go straight to the semifinals," I said.

"And if we lose, we're still okay. We still have you and Aaron out there as *teammates*." He emphasized the word.

I got what he was trying to say. I wasn't going to cause any problems. We'd get along tonight and for two or three more games. All bets were off after that.

"Let's see how we start, Jordan. If it's not working, I'll sub off Tammy and put you back on guard," Coach said.

"She's going to be good. You'll see."

The ref blew the whistle. We'd soon find out if I was right.

I jogged onto the court, passing my mom, who was seated a few feet away from some other mothers, her legs crossed and her foot tapping. I joined the starters as the rest of our players went to the bench.

Walking out, I caught sight of my dad at the far end of the bleachers in his usual place. He was hard to miss, a large figure by himself. I had kind of hoped he wasn't going to come at all. He'd noticed that I was looking his way, and he touched his fingers against his chest before pointing them at me. Coach yelled for us to come over, so I didn't have to return the gesture. I turned and ran to the huddle. I decided not to look in my dad's direction for the rest of the game.

Tammy leaned in to me. "I'm nervous. I don't want to let everyone down."

"You'll be great," I said quietly to her.

"But you don't have anything to prove," she whispered back.

Didn't I? It was because of me we were down two players—two *starters*. I was the one who should feel nervous. I was the one who had to show Aaron and everyone else that I could carry this team if I had to. At least, we'd soon find out if I could.

There were still almost seven minutes left in the game, but we didn't seem to be able to close the gap. We had struggled to get as close as one point, but the other team's lead had risen to six in the short time Coach had put the starters on the bench to take a break. It was probably smart—if it didn't last longer than another minute, that is. We needed to get back out there.

I stood up and walked toward Coach as he called a time-out. He turned to the bench. "Starters back in."

We gathered around him.

"You're going to play all of the last seven minutes," he said. "Jordan, you have to be careful. We need you out there, and you only have one more foul before you're gone."

"Yeah, pass more," Aaron snapped. "There's no *I* in *team*."

"As far as I know, there's no *I* in *covered* either. Get open more, and you'll get more passes."

"I'm open. We're all open."

"Everyone look for the open man—um, person. Sorry, Tammy."

She nodded. She was tired, but she hadn't stopped playing hard. The other team had been pushing on her, pressing whenever she had the ball. They weren't about to let a girl show them up, and she'd been playing her heart out. I'd been playing my heart out too. I had twenty-six points—a season high. I'd never needed to score so many points before because there were always other options.

"Let's go with the set high-post play on the inbounds," Coach said.

That was a good play—if Junior was the guard. Tammy was playing well, but she was no Junior, and she didn't have his experience or intuition. The play wasn't going to work well without him. We walked onto the court to take our positions, but now Tammy was the curling guard and Jing was throwing the inbounds pass.

As soon as we set up the play, it was obvious from their defense that the other team was looking for it. I trotted toward Jing on the sidelines.

"Fake to Tammy and throw it to me down on the low block."

He nodded.

The ref handed him the ball, and I ran to the low block. I glanced up and saw my dad in the stands. He wasn't alone anymore. Beside him was a large man—probably the only person actually bigger than him. Brodie. He'd brought Brodie to my game! I glowered up at them. My dad had his hand on Brodie's bicep.

The ball came whistling toward me, and I got my hands up just in time to grab it. I faked left, spun and put up a shot off the backboard and through the hoop. I was fouled hard, knocked over. The ref blew the whistle. I bounced back to my feet. I had a chance to make it into a three-point play and cut the lead in half in under five seconds.

I went to the line as both sides got into position. The ref handed me the ball. I bounced it a couple of times and tried to focus on the hoop. Instead my eyes went farther. Back up into the stands to my father and Brodie. They were there, side by side, looking down at me getting ready to take the shot. My dad still had his hand on Brodie's arm, gripping him.

I forced my mind back to the court. I bounced the ball twice, spun it and bounced it again. Exactly the way I always did, the way my dad had taught me. The ball blurred and went out of focus as my eyes moved to the stands again.

"Come on, son, take your shot," the ref called out.

I shot the ball. It bounced off the front of the rim. There was a scramble. Aaron came up with the ball and put up a shot. It rolled around the rim and missed! We all scrambled for the rebound. I grabbed the ball at the same time as one of their players. I ripped it from his arms and threw it back up. It dropped!

I heard the crowd scream, my dad's voice above all the others. I didn't care. I wasn't doing this for him. I wasn't putting on a show for him and his *boyfriend*. I saw the gymnasium doors open and my mom walking toward the exit. She turned and looked up into the bleachers. My dad was beaming, both hands on Brodie's arm. Brodie took my dad's hands and slid them off. He leaned into my dad and whispered something in his ear. My father clapped. I looked back toward my mom. She was gone.

I forced my mind back onto the court and into the game. "Everybody on defense!" I yelled as I ran down the court.

They put up a basket, and it dropped. Not good, but we were still four points up with less than twenty seconds on the clock. They needed two possessions to get a tie or a win. They didn't retreat onto defense. They were going to go for the steal, and if that didn't work, the foul. I took the ball from Jing.

"Go long," I said to Jing. "Tammy, inbound the ball," I called out.

"But—"

"Baseball pass. Look for me, Aaron or Jing."

She stepped out-of-bounds and took the ball from me.

"Let me do it!" Aaron said. He grabbed the ball away from Tammy.

I snatched the ball back from him. "I want somebody I can trust to do the throw-in."

"It's okay if he wants to," Tammy said.

"It isn't what he wants, it's what—" I stumbled forward. Aaron had shoved me! He'd come up behind me and pushed me right in the back.

"Think of what's good for the team and stop being such a girl," Aaron said.

Without thinking, I turned and threw the ball right at him. He dodged, and the ball glanced off the side of his head, then hit the wall. His eyes got big and glassy before he blinked and gritted his teeth. Aaron rushed forward as the ref blew his whistle repeatedly and then stepped in between us.

"What are you two doing?" the ref demanded. "That's a foul!"

"Time-out!" Coach called. "Both of you, to the bench!"

Aaron didn't move, and I wasn't going to be the first one to go.

"Do it now or you're both off the team."

We grumbled, but we moved. The ref followed us over to the bench, where Ms. Jones, along with Junior, was already waiting.

"I'm giving them both a technical. They're both gone for fighting!" the ref snapped.

"You can't do that," Junior said.

"Do you want a tech too?"

"No offense, sir, but the fighting rule is for fighting with somebody on the *opposition's* team. They were fighting each other. And I'm only a spectator today."

"Junior's right," my father said. He had suddenly materialized, standing behind Junior. "You can give a bench foul for delay of game, but you can't give them technical fouls for fighting or toss them."

"You sure about that, Chris?" the ref asked. It was no surprise that he and my dad knew each other or that he wanted my father's opinion.

"No question, Glen. And really, they didn't fight. My son threw a really, really bad pass."

The ref laughed. "Do you expect me to believe that?"

My dad winked.

"Okay, one shot then." Glen turned to Coach. "Get your team under control or it's another bench foul." He turned back to my dad. "Right?"

Dad nodded.

Without having said anything, Ms. Jones returned to the stands. My dad stayed behind the bench.

Brodie came up behind him. "I'm going to go."

Dad turned to touch Brodie's arm again, but Brodie moved out of his reach.

"Stay."

"We'll talk later." Brodie inclined his head almost imperceptibly toward me as he turned and left.

"Ethan and Ryan, you're in," Coach said. He looked down at Aaron and me on the bench. "The game is over for you two. Actually, your *season* may be over."

Twenty-Two

"What were you thinking?" Tammy demanded, coming at me as I exited the change room.

"Aaron shoved me."

"And you threw a ball at my brother's head."

"You slapped him this morning."

"Well, I shouldn't have. We can't have another starter sitting out. You need to put aside your feelings and do what's best for the team."

"You think I wasn't?"

"I don't know, Jordan."

"We're in the playoffs, aren't we? We have a bye, right?"

Tammy shook her head. Suddenly my dad came up behind me.

"Tammy, I'd offer you and your brother a ride, but I think we should keep the two of them apart right now," he said.

"Thanks for the offer. It's not far. I'd rather walk." She turned to me. "We'll talk more about this later."

Great. Something else to look forward to.

"Let's go, Jordan," my dad said.

"I'd rather walk too."

"You can't walk to my place."

"Who said I'm going to your place?" I demanded.

"Me and your mom. She left the gym but not the building."

"Is she okay?"

"She asked me to take you tonight."

Without saying another word, I turned and walked away.

"Jordan!" my dad called after me.

"I'm going to the car," I yelled without turning around.

I was steps ahead of my dad the entire time. We got into the Camaro and closed the doors.

"Jordan, I don't understand what you were thinking."

"You don't understand what I was thinking? What about you?"

"What do you mean?"

"What was Brodie doing here?"

He looked sheepish. "Brodie didn't think he should come either."

"He got that right." I took a deep breath. "Hey, what did Ms. Jones and Mr. Tanner say to you after the game?"

"We're going to have a bigger meeting next week with them, Aaron's parents and Mrs. Mercer."

"Am I suspended?"

"I don't think either of you will be. No guarantees. We talked about what you're going through. I think they understand how hard all this is for everyone."

I didn't think *anybody* really understood, least of all my dad. His boyfriend got it more than he did. Brodie hadn't wanted to be there. Despite that, he'd still shown up.

"This might be your last chance. I can't keep getting called in because of your behavior."

"What about your behavior?" I asked. "Your hands were all over your *boyfriend*." I spit the last word out.

"You're right. Brodie was right. He thought we might be making you uncomfortable," my dad said. "I'm just trying to be the person I am. I'm not expecting you to take on the job of defending me. You can't fight everybody who says something."

"I don't have a choice. You're my dad." I scowled at him, and if I'd had a ball, I'd have thrown it at his head to see the same glazed look on his face as on Aaron's. Maybe throwing a ball at his head was the only way he'd see what I'd been facing lately.

My dad started the engine. He glanced around quickly, without adjusting his mirrors or putting on his flashers, and barely stepped on the brakes as we sailed out of the school parking lot.

He rolled through stop signs, my body swaying as he took corners, until we were on the highway and soaring out of Franklin. My dad shifted gears. The Camaro leaped along like a happy puppy, leash in mouth, as he took it up. Then he let it glide. We coasted along, the Camaro almost not touching the ground. I was feeling uneasy, uncomfortable, maybe even a little scared. Why was he driving this way, and where was he taking us? This wasn't the way to his place.

"Where are we going?" I asked.

"We're here."

My dad shifted down, and the car shuddered. We bumped off the road into a dusty parking lot and came to a sudden stop. He flipped on the high beams and got out of the car, striding up the driveway through an overgrown field to a ramshackle old garage with boards missing and the door rusting out. Why were we here? I didn't want to go with him, but it was even worse to sit there alone. I got out and followed. The asphalt we walked on had big chunks coming up, the cracks filled in with tall, thin grass, most of the blades dried out and brown.

I caught up to my dad as he lifted the garage door. It squealed a complaint as he hoisted it. It only went up three-quarters of the way.

"Where are we?" I asked quietly. It looked like some-where out of a horror film, moths and other bugs crossing in front of the headlamps, the sound of crickets the only noise.

"Your grandfather's garage," my dad said. "His workshop."

"This is nowhere near his old place."

"No, it isn't." My dad ducked and went inside.

Afraid to stay outside alone, I ducked under the door too. The space was big enough for at least two trucks. Moonlight leaked in from holes in the roof where it looked like some animal had tried to get in. I could see the studs and what remained of the outer walls, and two wooden sawhorses, one farther along in falling apart than the other. An old calendar hung off a bent nail sticking out of the wall. Through the dust that covered the paper I could see a topless woman in just a bikini bottom and high heels, leaning over the hood of a red muscle car.

"Who owns this place now?" I asked.

"I guess me. I pay the property taxes. The land is virtually worthless. I haven't been here for years and didn't think I'd ever be back." My dad walked up to the calendar. It looked like he was going to rip it down, but he lowered his hand and left it. "This was where your grandfather brought broken things to fix."

"Did he fix them?"

"Sometimes. Usually the parts got salvaged and turned into something new. He'd Frankenstein a toaster plug onto a vacuum cord to get a kettle working again. Or at least he'd try."

"But why are we here?"

My father stood under the biggest hole in the roof. He closed his eyes and inhaled. "Because I tried to leave a lot of broken things behind and ended up carrying them with me. And because I don't want you to carry them with you. I guess I came here to tell you a story."

"Can't we do this back in the car?"

My dad still had his eyes closed. "The car's actually part of it. It's part of the inheritance. Let's sit outside while we talk."

He left the space, me close behind him, and lowered the garage door as far back down as it would go.

He sat on the asphalt and leaned back against the door. He tried to cross his legs and winced a little as his right knee disagreed. I took a spot beside him and began picking at the grass and swatting at bugs that tried to land on me.

"This is where I found the Camaro," my dad started. "It's where your grandfather hid it. I thought he'd sold it or destroyed it. I guess he did leave it to be destroyed. It was almost completely a junker, but the frame was still good. I knew I could salvage it, restore it."

"I know this story," I said as I ripped up a clump of grass.

"Maybe not this part," he said. "I used to drive the Camaro around with a friend of mine. We'd come out here. We'd fallen for each other, and we thought things were okay. But we weren't as careful or discreet as we thought. Your grandfather found out and followed us."

I stopped pulling up grass. "Is this story going to get gross?"

He continued as if he hadn't heard me. "Your grandfather never really saw anything, and I never admitted to anything, but I figure he knew. He told me that it was time to become a man and make some decisions about my life. That I had some choices to make. We never talked about it again, and I never saw my friend again. I put that all away—or at least tried to.

"And I realize now how much I've lived my life feeling like I'm being watched. So I put on the show. I tried to be the person who could have all the things he wanted in life, someone worth watching. I didn't realize your grandfather did the same thing. And everyone saw through it anyway.

"I practiced twice as hard, played even harder on the courts and ended up busting my knee. And your mom was there, and she was just so perfect. She made so much sense. I got married. I took the job, got a promotion, had a family. But none of it worked, Jordan. Nothing I could do was ever good enough for your grandfather. In the end he even hated that I was one of the guys giving orders instead of one of the *real* men producing things. Your mom and I looked good, but it was always so much work."

"What does this all mean, Dad?"

He pulled his knees up to his chest. "It means I don't want to leave you with a falling-apart garage in the middle of nowhere and an old Camaro and the belief that it's more important to be who you think people want you to be. That it's okay to be deeply unhappy with who you are. I know you don't want to hear this, but I think I can be happy with Brodie. Don't be the person who spends his life pretending and getting in the way of his own happiness, Jordan. I'm tired of pretending."

We sat for a while against the old garage door, just two buffets for the nighttime insects. I began to think about broken things. I began to think about the people who break them. If this garage ever became mine, I'd tear it to the ground, rip up the asphalt, let the tall grasses have every piece of the dump and erase all signs of what was here.

Finally my dad stretched and stood up. "We should head back. It's getting late."

Twenty-Three

I followed my dad into his apartment, but it wasn't the apartment I'd last seen. An actual bed on a frame was set up. There were curtains on the windows and rugs on the floor, and the tiny television was on a stand.

Dad hung his keys on one of the hooks on the wall.

"It's not finished yet. I hope you like what I've done to the place," my dad said as he switched on some lights. "There's a space for you over here."

He crossed over to a couch that looked like it was made from wooden slats. "It's a futon," he said as he wrestled with the back. He slid it down so the whole thing became a bed. "I'll get some bedding while you get cleaned up."

I kept thinking I'd be resting my head where everyone else had rested their butts. I went to the washroom.

"There's an extra toothbrush under the sink for you," my dad called through the door.

The towels were pink and had flowers embroidered on them. I recognized them as ones my mom had brought home from work a few months earlier. There were already two toothbrushes in the holder beside the sink.

"It's okay, right?" my dad asked when I came out of the bathroom. The bed was made. "I've been trying to make it better. Brodie's sister-in-law did a renovation—Brodie told me that you and I couldn't live like two broke frat boys and that I needed a grown-up apartment."

"Sure. It's fine. Whatever."

"This is what I've got for now."

I looked down at the futon, then sat on the edge and began to flip through the CDs and DVDs stacked on the shelf below the television.

"Those are mostly Brodie's."

"There's only one good movie. *Die Hard.* All the rest are chick flicks," I commented. I flipped over a boxed set of CDs called *Pride Anthems* with songs by Gloria Gaynor, ABBA, Celine Dion, Shania Twain and Cher. Brodie's taste was, so far, not great. "Does he like these, or did he not want them anymore?"

My dad ignored my comment. "The futon is pretty comfortable. I've dropped off on it a few times. You can watch TV if you want to fall asleep to it. Otherwise, it's late, so lights out."

I left the TV off and slid under the blankets. I listened to my dad getting ready in the bathroom before he padded across the floor and got into bed.

"Jordan?" he said across the room. "Despite how things went down earlier tonight, I'm glad you're here."

I rolled over so my back was to him and didn't answer.

I woke up to the smell of bacon and bread. I knew what those smells were before I opened my eyes, before I realized I wasn't at home but at my dad's over-the-garage apartment.

I propped myself up on an elbow and looked over to my dad's bed. It was made, the cover pulled tight and the pillows plump against the headboard. The bathroom door opened and a cloud of steam escaped, followed by Dad.

"Morning," he said. "All yours. Be quick. Breakfast's almost ready."

I went to the washroom and came back out when I'd finished brushing my teeth and getting dressed in the same clothes I'd changed into after the game.

"Your stuff is in the wash. The machines are down in the garage," my dad said. He held out a plate piled high with scrambled eggs, sausages and what looked like biscuits. "We'll have to eat standing at the counter."

"Where's the bacon?" I asked.

My dad smiled. "Try the scones."

I broke off a piece from one. It was incredibly flaky, with bits of bacon, chives and old cheddar. It had a kick to it.

"These are really good, Dad," I said. "But what am I eating?"

"I was playing around with scones and biscuits, though kitchen space is pretty limited. And I found this old recipe for this thing sort of like a biscuit, sort of like a scone, that used butter and pork lard. I figured I'd add bacon and stuff and a little jalapeño for heat."

"I'd stop playing around now. These are really good. Can I get another?" I asked, holding out my plate.

"Sure. But eat your eggs and sausages too. After we wash up, what do you think about playing some ball?"

I almost blurted out that all I really wanted to do was go home and be left alone. I looked over at Dad waiting for my answer. His expression was so hopeful. I thought about how many times we'd played ball together. It was something we both loved, something we shared…and a way not to talk about anything except the game.

"We can play if you don't mind that I'm going to school you," I said.

"You think you've suddenly gotten better in the last couple of weeks?"

"Not only did I get better, but you got older."

"Has Junior been helping you with your trash talk?"

"It's not talk if you back it up. You'll see."

After breakfast we washed the dishes, which it turned out had belonged to us before too. My dad ran down to put my uniform in the dryer, and I went out to the driveway. I warmed up with a few free throws. There was a new net hanging from the rim, as he had promised.

"You might want to keep some clothes here," Dad said as he came out the garage's side door. "You know you can keep whatever you want here. I want it to feel like your space too."

I didn't answer because it would have meant telling my dad that his apartment would never feel like my space, not with Brodie's old stuff all over or me sleeping on a couch in the same room as my dad and the kitchen. It wasn't even really my dad's space. It was a sad room above a garage that no grown man should have been living in. In fact, I could imagine my mom saying just that.

"One-on-one, Horse or twenty-one?" Dad asked, bouncing the ball over to me.

"Definitely one-on-one."

"Usual rules?"

"Sounds good."

Since my father was a lot taller and bigger than me, we had rules to make the game more competitive. He was only allowed one offensive rebound per play. If he missed twice, the ball became mine. More important, he wasn't allowed to back me down in the low post. If he did that, there was no way I could ever stop him.

Over the years, as I'd gotten bigger and better, the rules changed. When I was really little, they were things like he wasn't allowed in the key, couldn't get rebounds or could only shoot left-handed hook shots. So when we played, it was a real game. He played hard and I played hard, and if I won, it was fair.

"And remember, practice how you play," he said.

I began slowly, feeling my dad out. We hadn't played in a while, and my dad was a little rusty, but I also knew he'd pick up quickly the longer we played. I drove at him, going hard into his right-hand side, knowing it was his weak one. I pivoted, faked, changed directions and darted around his left side, knowing his knee wouldn't let him turn quickly. I put it up and sank it.

I led in points, the morning sun warming us as my dad warmed up too. It wasn't long before he began to close the gap, and soon we were tied.

"Prepare to eat it," I said to my dad, dribbling.

"I already figured out you're targeting my right," he replied. "I'm onto you."

I smiled at him, still dribbling, and then dashed down his left side.

I heard two horn honks. Dad straightened up. I went past him with not even an attempt to stop me as I scored.

I retrieved the ball. Dad was walking toward the end of the driveway, a familiar big red truck sitting there. Brodie went around the back of it and lowered the tailgate.

"What about the game?" I called out.

"How's it going?" Brodie waved.

Reluctantly I sauntered down to them.

"Aren't you supposed to be at your cabin this weekend?" my dad asked.

"I was on my way when a restaurant buddy called with a lead on a place closing. Owners are retiring. I picked you up something." Brodie unstrapped some ratchet tie-downs and pulled back a tarp.

I peeked into the back of the truck. There was a long wooden table.

"So you can get back to your baking," Brodie said. "I know you were missing it."

"Seriously? But I can't be spending money on that now."

"Do you like it?"

"I love it, but—"

"It's a loan. They don't make utility tables like this anymore, and my shop doesn't have room. Everything about it was too good for me to pass up. You can use it until I clear some space or move into a bigger location."

My dad threw his arms around Brodie's neck. "I love it," he repeated. "It's going to be the perfect island, and it will divide the kitchen area from the rest of the apartment. And if I find some stools, I can have seating. I love it. Thank you."

Brodie looked at me over my dad's shoulder. He took a step back.

"You two grab one end and head up the stairs," Brodie said. "Go slow at the top before we turn."

"But the game," I said.

"We'll finish up once we get this into the apartment," Dad replied. "I'll be able to knead bread again."

"I offered him a bread machine I've never used," Brodie said. "Still new in the box."

"He'd never take that. It doesn't let him—"

"Feel the dough," Brodie said, finishing my sentence.

The table was heavier than I'd expected. I didn't know how Brodie was supporting one end of it by himself. He was right—the swing to get it into the apartment wasn't fun, but he seemed fine, almost lifting it by himself at some points and suspending it over the railing while from inside we maneuvered it into the apartment.

"It's perfect," my dad said as we stood back, all of us sweaty. It did make the space look more like separate rooms. More like an actual apartment someone might live in rather than a place above a garage.

"I'll get going," Brodie said. "If I leave now, I'll get to the cabin before dark."

"Do you have to go right away?" my father asked. "Let me pack you some of those scones. I made them again so Jordan could try them."

"Are we going to finish playing?" I cut in.

My dad rubbed his shoulder as he rotated it. "You're not tired? If only I were thirteen again."

Brodie laughed, all bass drum. "Not me. Never again. Thirteen was rough, really rough."

We headed back down to the driveway, and I bounce-passed the ball to my dad. "Let's go," I said.

"Brodie, you could stay and play even for a few minutes," my dad said. "You can play the winner."

"Another time. I'm not dressed for it."

"I can lend you something, unless you're afraid to lose."

"I really need to get on the road, Chris."

"Be a sport," my dad replied. "At least stay and watch for a minute."

"Just a minute."

My father tossed me the ball and I dribbled, trying to turn the corner, but he slid over and blocked the way. I crossed to go up the other side. He was there before me. My father was suddenly taking this game more seriously, or his knee had somehow stopped hurting. Was he showing off for Brodie?

I faked in, drew back out and then drove to my dad's right side, got around him, aimed and released. A hand shot over me and sent the ball shooting across the driveway!

Brodie palmed the ball as it bounced toward him. He underhand-tossed it to me. "I really do need to get going," he said.

"Okay." My dad seemed a bit sad. "I'll walk you to your truck."

They went down the driveway with room left between them. It made me remember Donavan's mom at the dance.

My dad stretched up, and for a second I thought they were going to kiss. Brodie placed a hand against my father's chest. He gave a nod in my direction, and I heard him say, despite his trying to whisper, "Not now. I'll call you on my way back in on Sunday." He waved at me with those monster hands. "Catch you later, Jordan!"

My dad had his head down as he walked back up the driveway.

"Ready?" he asked.

I shook my head. I didn't want to play ball. Somehow even this had been ruined. "I want to take a shower. And I've got homework."

"It's Saturday, Jordan. You can do it tonight or tomorrow."

"I want to clean up. I'm tired. I don't want to play." I tossed him the ball.

"You must be tired if you're turning down basketball.

I'll get your uniform out of the dryer, then wash the clothes you've got on."

I went up the stairs and walked inside. This wasn't my home. If I were at home I'd have a dresser full of clothes and would be able to toss my sweaty stuff into a hamper. At home I wouldn't see my father almost kiss his boyfriend. I wanted to go home and play ball with Junior or ride my bike over to Ridge Town and figure out what was going on between Tammy and me. Even if my dad tried to make space for me here, and even if he got new furniture or towels or an actual bed for me, it would always be a space Brodie had marked. There would always have been two toothbrushes in the holder first and an extra for me under the sink. There was no place for me or my toothbrush here.

Twenty-Four

Ms. Jones and Mrs. Mercer intercepted me before I had a chance to get to my first class.

"Jordan! A word!" Ms. Jones called across the students hurrying to get to class before the bell sounded.

"I'll be late," I said.

"I've spoken to Miss Morrison," Ms. Jones said. "She knows you're going to miss first period. Let's go to my office."

"If this is about the game," I said, "I thought it was settled. It was an accident. My dad explained that."

Mrs. Mercer smiled. "Let's talk in private," she suggested. "I think that would be easier."

I rolled my eyes. "What kind of privacy do you think I've been getting lately? If you're going to punish me, can you just do it and let me get on with my day?"

Ms. Jones said, "Okay. We'll talk here. I understand what happened at the game, and I understand what you've been going through."

"I don't think you do."

Ms. Jones shook her head. "I'm not impressed with your attitude. Do we need to re-involve your parents and reconsider the consequences?"

"No. Sorry. No, ma'am."

"I probably don't fully understand what you're going through, but I was at the game and I saw what happened on the court and in the stands. I'm not about to let a student who is demonstrating a need for assistance have his needs ignored. Mrs. Mercer was brought in as a resource that I intend to utilize to the best of her abilities. And now, even more than before, I think we've made the correct decision that instead of weekly meetings, you'll have them every other day."

"But—" I said.

"But nothing. This is not a discussion. You'll meet with her during first period today. The rest of the week will be during lunch hours so your classes and practices aren't impacted. Do you have your things?"

"Yes, ma'am."

I walked with them flanking me past all the other classrooms, where attendance was about to be taken. It felt like everybody still in the halls was looking at me and trying not to get caught looking at me.

I turned my head. Through an open door I saw a girl poke Tammy and point at me. Tammy looked up. I tried to give her a smile but knew it was weak.

I started to follow Mrs. Mercer into the office, but Ms. Jones put a hand on my shoulder to stop me.

"Jordan," she said, "before you go in, you should know

it's Mrs. Mercer who's been one of the strongest advocates for your remaining on the basketball team. It's her belief that ending your season would be detrimental to you. I'm not sure, if it were up to me alone, that you'd be playing right now. I personally would not hesitate to kick you off the team, even this close to the championships. Are we unclear about anything?"

"No, ma'am."

"Have a good talk," Ms. Jones said. "I don't like what you're going through. I'm hoping we can improve this."

That was the first I'd heard that students got punished to make things easier on them. I didn't think so.

"You're welcome to leave the door open, but most people choose to close it," Mrs. Mercer said.

She was on a rolling office chair behind a desk, and she began to propel herself around the desk while seated. There was a chair with a padded vinyl seat and back for me. It was a small step up from those folding metal chairs we sometimes used during assemblies.

I pulled the door almost closed and took my seat, figuring this would be my usual spot until my punishment was lifted, a punishment that kept me on the basketball team and in school.

I placed both feet on the floor and intentionally folded my hands on my lap, remembering my resolve not to speak.

"I think we both know why you're here," Mrs. Mercer said.

I shrugged. "Yeah, I know." I went back to staring at Mrs. Mercer's forehead so it would look like I was looking at her when I wasn't.

Mrs. Mercer shifted in her rolling chair. "While Ms. Jones is concerned about the aggression toward other students, this is about helping you. We know that there's your parents separating…"

I forced myself to stare past her head, through it, imagining the wall behind her skull.

"…your father dating a new man, and a lot of other changes. Do you want to tell me how you're doing with all that?"

I shook my head.

"There's also your relationship with Tammy."

I broke my stare and looked at Mrs. Mercer, trying to read her expression. Did she care about Tammy and me, or was she just trying to get me talking?

"It seems that's going well."

I went back to staring past her. I knew the game. This was chicken. The first one to give in wasn't going to be me.

"Jordan." Mrs. Mercer sighed. "I really am on your side, but I can't help if you refuse to speak. Do you have anything you want to say?"

"My punishment was attending sessions with you. I wasn't told I had to talk or participate. Just attend."

Mrs. Mercer shrugged this time. "I'd like to think I'm more than a punishment."

I didn't respond. I wasn't going to give her that.

"I really would like to know what's going on and see if I can help you."

"You can't."

"I'm not in the business of forcing anyone to confide in me if they don't want to. But I can offer you tools and strategies that might help you. Your call." She leaned back in her chair and watched me.

I continued to stare past her. I wondered how long we could both sit here—if it was just through first period, I could wait her out until the bell sounded.

Finally Mrs. Mercer said, "I can't force you to tell me what's been going on or how you feel. I will be honest, though, and tell you that until Ms. Jones and I feel you are in a better place, these sessions will continue. They'll continue past the basketball season. Indefinitely. We are on your team, if you let us be."

Mrs. Mercer glanced at her watch. "The period is almost up. I'm going to let you go on one condition. I want you to think about ways we can work together. If you don't want to talk, that's okay. You can choose a method you like better. All right?"

"Sure. Thanks," I said. That last one was a trick too. A pretty good one. But it was still playing chicken, and Mrs. Mercer didn't know I was fine with the silence.

I hurried to Tammy's classroom door as soon as we were let out for lunch.

"Hey," she said as I trotted up to her, maneuvering through the crowd filling the hallways. "What was that earlier? Are you in trouble?"

"More sessions," I said. "I'm still on the team though."

Tammy faced me, holding one of her backpack straps with both hands. "Like I said after the game, I'm serious about wanting to talk." She went right for it.

"I didn't plan to bounce the ball off Aaron's head."

"I know. After slapping him, I understand wanting to hit him, believe me. You need to think about the team."

"Junior's back, Aaron's okay, and Donavan will return by the semis for sure. And I'm still on the team."

"You know you won't get another chance. You can't fight."

"Sometimes you need to fight. You should understand that better than anyone else around here," I said.

"I do. But sometimes you need to play it smart so you can fight the battles that matter. A basketball championship doesn't really matter."

"If that doesn't matter, what is it you think does?" I asked.

"You do."

I grinned. "I do?"

"Stop it."

"Are we good?"

"We haven't talked about what Aaron said to you."

"Do we have to?"

"We should talk about your father."

"Can't you let me handle my own dad?"

Tammy bit her bottom lip. "I guess."

"So we're good?"

"I guess."

I leaned in and pressed my lips firmly against Tammy's. The remaining kids still streaming past us hooted.

Tammy pushed me back. "We're in the middle of school in the middle of the hall in the middle of the day."

I leaned in and kissed her again quickly.

She smiled. "You're playing it dangerous. We could get in trouble." She slid her hand into mine as we began to walk down the hallway.

"I'm already in trouble. Maybe it will give Mrs. Mercer and me something to talk about." I took my hand from hers and slid it around her waist.

Tammy looked up at me and resumed holding her backpack strap with both hands as we walked, my hand on her hip.

When we sat down at the table of other basketball players, I moved my arm up across her shoulders.

Tammy pushed it off as she leaned in and whispered, "Not now. Not in front of the team." She held my hand under the table instead.

I darted in and kissed her cheek. Tammy blushed as the team, led by Junior, began *ooh*ing loudly.

"This is embarrassing," Tammy whispered.

"Aren't you happy to be my girlfriend?" I whispered back into her ear.

"Yes. Of course. But maybe cool it a little."

Just then Angelique walked by, carrying her tray. She leaned in close and said, "Nice win."

"We do our best," Aaron said. The others nodded and fist-bumped in agreement.

"You were amazing, J.R.," she added and offered a big smile.

As she walked away, Junior said, "I'm not sure that 'nice win' comment was aimed equally at everyone at the table."

Tammy pressed into me and pulled my arm back onto her shoulders. She reached up and held my hand and looked over at Angelique, who had taken her place at a table with other girls.

Twenty-Five

Tammy and I had been inseparable the next two days. Of course, every other lunch hour was only half as long for me now because the other half was devoted to reporting to Mrs. Mercer.

Tammy and I bumped our way down the hall. The lunch rush was always this way. Either the school needed wider hallways or fewer students. It felt like we were swimming upstream as almost everybody else headed to eat and we headed to the office. I'd told her she didn't really need to go with me, but I liked her being with me on the walk. I guess it would have been easier to make our way through the stream if we weren't holding hands, but I liked that too, so I wasn't letting go.

Tammy trailed behind. I was sort of like an icebreaker clearing a path for us through the onrushing crowd. Somebody bumped into me.

"Hey, watch where you're going!" I snapped.

"Sorry," he said. He was smaller, younger and probably in seventh grade.

"Watch yourself. Understand?"

He mumbled a second "sorry," lowered his head and slipped by us.

"Guy needs to be more careful," I said to Tammy.

"It was an accident. It's not like he did it on purpose."

Tammy yanked on my arm and pulled me into the shelter of a class doorway, out of the flow of the traffic. The room was empty. She let go of my hand.

"You can't afford to be in another fight."

"As far as I know, I haven't been in any *actual* fights."

"You know what I mean."

"That's ancient history—last week," I joked. "I got everything taken care of."

"If it's all taken care of, then why do you have to see Mrs. Mercer again today?"

"She's part of my punishment."

"They punish you with detentions and suspensions. She's here to help you."

When she said that, I wondered if she'd been talking to Ms. Jones or Mrs. Mercer.

"I don't need any help, and it's not like I have a choice. Three times a week until they're happy."

She took my hand again—which I liked—and pulled me into the empty classroom—which I didn't like.

"You need to slow down," she said.

"I wasn't moving that fast. He bumped into me."

"I don't mean how fast you were moving in the hall. I mean the way you've been acting."

"And how have I been acting?"

"You've been talking louder and arguing with people."

"There are lots of stupid people."

"That sounds like something Aaron would say."

"Okay, that stings."

"I'm not trying to hurt you. I'm trying to help." She paused. "Look, I know with the separation and your dad, it's hard."

It all kept coming back to him. It seemed like everybody knew about my father and had decided what was going on with me was a direct line back to him. I hated people thinking they knew everything about my life. They didn't know anything.

"Can we let it go? I said I was handling it."

Tammy chewed her bottom lip. "About that. I've got some, uh, good news for you. I spoke to Ms. Jones yesterday, and she gave me permission to start a GSA."

I shook my head. "Am I supposed to know what any of that means?"

She laughed, but it was a nervous one. "I guess I shouldn't be surprised. Things are so different here in Franklin. It almost feels like we're living in a time warp. A GSA is a gay-straight alliance. It's a club that offers a safe environment for LGBTQ+ students and their friends."

"What?"

"I know. I don't love the name either, but it's a step forward. It's more important this club exists than getting stuck on semantics."

"Why are you doing this?" I asked. I wasn't completely sure what she had said, but I didn't want to sound stupid asking.

"Well, I was almost shocked that our school didn't have one. Lots of schools have been doing it for years. It's not like there aren't any LGBTQ+ kids in this school. Working on averages and the number of students here, there could be seventy-five to a hundred students needing a safe space to be heard."

"No way there's that many. There's not that many gay anythings in Franklin."

"It's not only gay rights. It's gender identity and equality. It's human rights. It's hard to be yourself without a support system. It's not an easy thing."

I thought she was talking about my father. "How would you even know? And did you need to start a club for these imaginary students?"

"Just because you aren't seeing them doesn't mean they're imaginary," Tammy said. "Sometimes there's no way of telling, even with people you've known all your life."

Now she was *definitely* talking about my father.

"Well, I'm not gay."

Tammy's eyebrows drew in. "That's really not funny."

"It wasn't supposed to be. Why can't you mind your own business and let me handle my own stuff? That's what you agreed to."

"Alliances need allies. I was hoping you'd be one. Then we'd have two of the basketball team's captains as members."

For a split second I thought Tammy had gotten her brother to join. Then I asked, "Junior joined?"

"As soon as I asked him, he signed up. He wants to be there for you and your father and everybody else. I was hoping you would too."

"You thought wrong," I snapped. "I'm not one of your issues, and I don't want to be joining some gay club. It's not my job to make things good for my father or anybody else."

Tammy looked hurt but squared her jaw before she spoke. "This is about everyone, not only you. But, yes, I was trying to make things easier specifically for you." Despite her efforts to appear strong, she seemed to be close to tears.

"You want to make things easier for me? Then stop. Stop trying to make things easier. Mind your own business. No one asked you to be a gay-rights hero."

"I'm trying to help," Tammy said.

"I'm your boyfriend. I don't want to be some charity case. My family isn't some cause from that file folder of yours."

"That's not how I see you."

"Let this one go. You agreed to let me handle this. Call off the club."

She didn't answer.

"Come on. I can't be late for Mrs. Mercer." I reached out to take her hand.

She pulled it away. "That's another thing. We don't have to hold hands everywhere. We don't have to be attached at the hand. Or anywhere else."

"What?"

"It feels like…I don't know, like I'm a prop lately. Like I'm supposed to be there for you to hang yourself off, but I'm not supposed to think or do anything."

We stared at each other.

I said, "I'm going. Are you coming or not?"

"Not."

"I thought you were all about being supportive."

"That doesn't mean I support your garbage, Jordan. Do you get how you've been? I've tried to justify it and remember you're a nice guy who's struggling. Support works two ways. Maybe I got the idea for the GSA because of you, but, and I really hate to break it to you, this is a bigger deal than Franklin's basketball star, Jordan Ryker. Get over yourself."

I started to say something and then stopped—I knew I should keep my mouth shut. But I couldn't help myself.

"Me? Why don't you get over yourself? Do you really think everybody's sitting around waiting to be saved by you? You're not saving the world or anyone. So don't try to save me. I don't need any of this."

"What do you need then?"

"I thought I needed my girlfriend. But I really don't need your club. I don't need your support. And I don't know if I even need you."

Before she could say another word, I spun around and left. The hall was less busy now, but I kind of wanted somebody to bump into me. At least a suspension would get me out of here.

Mrs. Mercer was standing at her door waiting. She looked at me and then down at her watch. I knew I was, like, a minute late at the most.

"Hello, Jordan. It's good to see you."

"Yeah, sure."

"I take it you're not any happier to see me today than you were earlier this week."

"I don't have a choice," I said as I brushed by her and slouched in the chair where I had sat before. She closed the door and took her seat across from me.

"How are you doing today?"

"Great." I'd keep my answers as short as possible.

"You actually look upset."

It was that obvious? "Nope."

"Did you decide on a different approach for our sessions?" she asked.

I shrugged. I still felt like smashing into someone. "I didn't feel like doing your job for you."

Mrs. Mercer smiled. "Confrontation. That can work, if you think that will help fix things."

"You can't fix anything."

"Maybe I can't. But at least we're talking now."

I threw up my arms in mock defeat. "So far talking has only caused me more problems. People need to keep their business to themselves."

"People like your father?" she asked.

"People like him and my girlfriend. Or ex-girlfriend."

"You and Tammy broke up?"

I shook my head. "I don't even know. It just happened. She went and set up some stupid GSA club thing."

"A gay-straight alliance. That sounds like a caring thing for her to do to support you."

I shrugged. That was sort of what Tammy had been trying to say. "But she had no right."

"So you aren't happy about it."

"Would you be? Why does everything in my life have to revolve around what my father did to me?"

"To you?"

"Well, to me and my mom."

"And you think he did this thing to hurt you two?"

"It doesn't matter why he did it. It still hurt us."

"And the thing he did was leaving you?"

I rolled my eyes as hard as I could. "Leaving and being gay."

"Oh, that. Well, what was his alternative?" she asked. "To stay and continue denying who he is?"

"Yes!" I practically yelled.

She looked at me for a long time before finally speaking. "Do you really think he did this *to* you and your mother or *for* himself?"

I wasn't really sure what she was trying to get at. It seemed like a lot of the things done recently had been done by my father, for my father. So I said, "Even if it was for him, it impacts us. He changed everything."

"But you believe he had a choice? Or, rather, that he made a choice?"

"I don't know. He could have waited or something."

"Hasn't he already 'waited or something'? Weren't your parents married a long time?"

She was speaking, but I was hearing the almost-identical words Junior had said to me.

"If he'd waited that long, why couldn't he have waited another few years?" I asked.

"How long would have worked for you?"

"I don't know. When I got into college? At least then I wouldn't be stuck in this town dealing with it. I could have lived my life, and he could have lived his."

"You wanted him to keep pretending for five more years?" she asked.

"I don't know."

"And that would be better?"

"Maybe."

"Better for you or for him?"

"For everybody. For me. For my mom. For him."

"So it would have been easier had your dad waited, and you all could have been a happy family until then?"

I thought about how we hadn't been a happy family for a long time. What we had been was a good act, but only if you looked from a distance. I remembered when I just wanted them to stop fighting. I'd gotten my wish. They weren't fighting anymore.

"There's nothing you can say and nothing some stupid school club can do for me," I said. "Everyone needs to stop wasting my time and their own."

"And that makes you angry."

"Wouldn't you be?" I demanded.

"I believe I would." She paused. "Maybe that's why you've been getting into fights with people. Because you're angry."

The bell that ended lunch rang. I jumped from my seat.

I'd been reckless. I'd said too much. "I have to get going. I don't want to be late for class."

Mrs. Mercer smiled. "You can stay. I can write a note."

I stood. "I don't need to stay. I did my time, right?"

"Then thanks for coming. I'll see you at our next session."

I was at the door and had it partway open when Mrs. Mercer said, "But if you do need to talk before then, you can ask Ms. Jones to get in touch with me. Even if you just want to have another fight and whittle away the time you're doing."

"Right. See you later."

Twenty-Six

"You ready?" I asked Junior. I grabbed my gym bag.

Junior gestured to himself. "Born ready. Let's go."

"Good practice, guys," Aaron said as we walked by.

Both Junior and I exchanged a low five with Aaron as we passed and left the change room.

"It's nice to see you two getting along better these days," Junior said.

"I wasn't the one who punched him in the face."

Junior laughed. "We both knew it was me instead of you because I'm faster on my feet. I'm the hare to your tortoise. Just saying."

"You're quicker, but you're not swifter. The hare didn't win. Remember?"

As we walked across the gym, Tammy came out of the other change room. She nodded toward us but kept walking.

"Is there some rule that you're only allowed to get along with one member of that family at a time?"

"Not a rule, but it seems to go down that way."

"If that's the case, I'd rethink things and go back to being on the outs with Air and on the ins with Tam. Catch up and go punch him. I'll wait."

"I don't think punching Aaron would make things better," I said.

"Too bad. You and Tam were just *sooooo* cute together. Puppy-dog, furry-kitten, baby-unicorn cute."

"Shut up."

"Walking around hand in hand like you were glued together—"

"Shut up."

"Sitting together, your arm over her. That look of young love. The sparks flying, both of you glowing and—"

"*Please*, shut up."

He stopped. "Now was that so hard, showing some manners?"

"No, not that hard."

We got to our lockers and tossed in our gym bags.

"Do you want to come over after school, play some hoops and join us for dinner?" I asked.

"You and your mom?"

"No one else is going to join us."

"Tammy might if you asked her," Junior said.

I gave him a questioning look.

"She hasn't really given up on you. At least, not yet."

I pulled some books out. "What makes you think that?"

"Look who you're talking to. I have my black belt in

understanding girls. I am wizard of women, a ninja of knowl-edge, a PhD of—you get the idea."

"What do you actually know?"

"I heard that somebody asked her out, and she wasn't interested."

"Not being interested in that person doesn't mean she's still interested in me. She's hardly talked to me in two days."

"That doesn't mean she hasn't talked about you to me." Junior slammed his locker shut and slipped on the lock. "You could get back together, assuming you apologize and don't do anything else stupid."

"Stupid? Like what?"

"Stupid like Angelique."

Angelique had been around and was now everywhere I'd turned since Tammy and I had broken up. Junior and I had walked Angelique partway home after school the day before, and she'd told me I could text her if I wanted to talk. She had taken my phone and put her number into it.

"Does she still want you to come to her house?" Junior asked.

"She made the team. She asked for my help improving her game."

"She's a guard. If it was her game she wanted improved, she would have talked to me."

"Maybe you should show her your moves then," I suggested.

"She couldn't handle them. Besides, she's not my type."

"And your type is?"

"Somebody not so desperate she's willing to date you."

"Funny. So wise ninja of women—"

"That's wizard of women, ninja of knowledge," he said, cutting me off.

"Apologies. Seriously, what do you think I should do?"

"Well, it's pretty obvious to everybody that Angelique is into you. She's nice, good-looking, and if you went out with her, you'd win the breakup."

"Huh?"

"First person to start dating somebody new is the winner. If you want to be the winner, ask Angelique out. Maybe even ask her to the semifinals game and give her a big hug and a kiss right in front of Tammy and—"

"I wouldn't do that."

"I know. So go tell Tammy you're sorry for what you did."

"But I didn't do anything!" I protested.

"Yeah, you did. She was trying to do something for you and for other people, the way she always does, and you reacted really badly."

"You weren't even there."

"She told me. Wasn't it like that?"

I almost started to argue but instead shook my head. I had been a jerk. And I hadn't realized how much Tammy was talking to Junior.

"Even if you don't think you were wrong, and, by the way, you were completely wrong, you need to apologize. Even better, come to the GSA meeting at lunch today."

"I don't know about that."

"I'm going. I could take you by the hand and lead you, since you like walking around holding somebody's hand so much."

"Not your hand. I don't want to go, and you don't have to go either just because Tammy decided to do this."

"I want to be part of it. It's about time our school had a GSA."

"Maybe. But only if you take my dad out of the equation. Tammy said there could be, like, seventy-five or more kids in our school who need her club."

"That's reassuring," Junior said.

"Reassuring?"

"Nobody should have to go through difficult stuff alone."

I thought back to when Junior had lost his father and how hard that had been and how I hadn't known what to say to him back then.

"Think how this must be for your dad," Junior said.

"I told you to take him out of it. All I hear about is how hard things are for him."

"Wouldn't it be easier if you weren't making yourself miserable all on your own?" Junior paused. "Being part of the GSA is sort of like being on a team, and your teammates have your back."

I couldn't stop myself from laughing. "Yeah, that describes our team *so* well."

Junior smiled. "Okay, not our *specific* basketball team, but a normal team. You have to admit that on the court we're pretty good. Except for you tossing the ball at Aaron's head, although who am I to talk, since I punched him in the face. Come to think of it, maybe you shouldn't try to get back together with Tammy."

"Really?"

"Yeah, I think she's too good for you. The girl deserves an upgrade." He tapped himself on the chest.

"You got to stop with the mixed messages," I said. "Either she deserves an upgrade or she deserves you."

He chuckled and offered me a high five. "Okay, that was good."

"Thanks. I learned from the best."

"It looks like I should have punched you instead of Aaron. It was a mistake to make bad blood with my future brother-in-law." Junior laughed again.

"It's good that at least one of us thinks you're funny."

"Funny? I'm hilarious," he said. "You know I'd never ask Tammy out, right? You're my best friend. I've got your back."

"Same."

"Really?" he asked.

"You have doubts?"

He shook his head. "None. You're like my brother. We're always there for each other, no matter what."

"No matter what," I agreed.

Junior had been there for me through all of this, even when I was the one who'd turned away. He was, and always would be, my best friend. I knew it and so did he. We were ride or die.

"I would never date Tammy. Not just because you're my best friend, but she's really not my type either."

I wanted to ask more, but the bell sounded.

Twenty-Seven

I walked back and forth outside the classroom designated for the GSA meeting. As much as I didn't want to go in, Junior was right. If I didn't, there was probably no chance of getting back together with Tammy. Even if we didn't get back together, I needed things good again between us. But if I went in, wasn't I basically putting a target on myself for guys like Aaron to keep saying stuff to me?

Junior stuck his head out the door. "What are you doing? Come inside."

Tammy was sitting behind the teacher's desk, head down, writing notes. She hadn't noticed me. Ms. Jones, the staff sponsor, was sitting on the windowsill. Other than Junior and me, no one else was in attendance.

"Shall we get started?" Ms. Jones asked.

Tammy let out a big sigh. "I was hoping there'd be more—" She looked up. "Jordan!"

"Uh, hey," I said. "I'm here for your club."

"It's not my club."

"Okay, I'm here for *the* club." I slid into a seat.

"I really was hoping there'd be more people," Tammy said.

"Don't be discouraged, Tammy," Ms. Jones said. "The club is new and hasn't built up any traction. Word still needs to get out."

"I shouldn't have expected more," Tammy replied. "We barely had time to get organized."

"Why don't we look at this as a brainstorming session?" Ms. Jones suggested, sliding off the windowsill and into a desk. "Why don't we talk about what we envision for the future of this club?"

"I've made a bullet-point agenda," Tammy said. "The first thing will be recruiting new members."

"That's a good place to start," Junior agreed.

Mrs. Mercer knocked on the open door. "I heard about a meeting. Can I still join you?"

"Please," Ms. Jones said. "We were discussing what we hope to see from this club. Does anybody have any thoughts?"

Junior pulled a folded-up piece of paper from the pocket of his jeans. "A few. I looked online, and one website said teachers could put up a sign or something and designate their classrooms as positive spaces."

"I like that," Mrs. Mercer said. "I hope you don't mind, but I'd like to suggest that to my other schools. Ideally every space is a positive space."

"*Ideally*," Tammy repeated, emphasizing the word. "Except we don't live in an ideal world."

I snorted a little.

"Jordan?" Ms. Jones asked.

"Is anything ideal?" I mumbled. Tammy stared at me. "We're here talking about what will make our school better for gay—"

"LGBTQ+," Tammy cut in.

"Okay, all of that," I said, knowing I risked reopening the fight that had caused our breakup, "but if we're part of a this kind of alliance, shouldn't there be some gay or other letter people in this room?"

"Who is in attendance doesn't undermine the importance of what Tammy, or we, are trying to do here," Ms. Jones said.

"It doesn't mean Jordan is wrong," Tammy added. "There's no alliance if it's one-sided. We're going to have to have more diverse members before anything else."

"Except you can't expect people to come in and, well, come out," Junior said.

Ms. Jones nodded. "No, no one will be forced to identify. That wouldn't work and would make some people hesitant or uncomfortable to join."

Tammy tapped her pen against her paper. "It feels like we're arguing and going nowhere."

"No one is arguing," I said. "I mean, no one is trying to. I thought we were trying to make things better."

"Maybe I didn't think this through enough before I came to you," Tammy said to Ms. Jones.

"It's a first meeting. I don't want any of us to give up on this," Ms. Jones said. "I can put you in contact with some colleagues who can offer advice on how to make this club more successful. For now let's keep having meetings. Maybe we can have some fun activities until we get rolling. Like watching a movie or TV show."

"I like that," Junior said. "No offense, but this meeting is kind of a drag. Oh, let's watch something about drag!"

Tammy looked down at her list. "There's still serious stuff we need to address."

"I promise we will," Ms. Jones said. "But it doesn't mean we can't have a little fun."

Tammy and I stared at each other. I didn't think either of us was having much fun.

"Feel free to use the classroom to finish up your lunches and continue discussing this." Ms. Jones stood and walked out the door.

"Good start," Mrs. Mercer said as she exited too.

Junior nearly jumped up. "Forgot my lunch in my locker," he squeaked and ran from the room.

Tammy stood and began stacking her papers.

I walked over to her.

"I didn't expect you to be here," she said without looking up at me.

"I didn't expect me to be here either. I wanted to see you. I wanted to make things good between us."

"Is that why you came?" Tammy finished stacking her papers.

"No, well, it was part of it, but not the whole reason. I wanted to talk to you and let you know I didn't mean what

I said before. At least, I didn't mean it the way I said it. I was upset. I know you're not being pushy and you just want to help people."

"Except I think you did mean some of it," Tammy replied. "And maybe you weren't wrong. But you weren't right either."

"I thought the two of us could go back to the way it was between us."

"Maybe we could start becoming friends again if the guy I liked shows up again."

"I'm here."

"Just because you're *here* doesn't mean you're *here*."

"Are you going to explain that?"

"You'll figure it out. Are you coming to the next meeting?"

"Yeah."

She gave me a smile. Not a full one—but it was something. "It's a good start. Thanks."

Twenty-Eight

Coach blew his whistle, and we all stopped running.

"Get a drink, then come back and take a knee."

It had been a fairly easy practice in terms of running but with a lot of discussion around plays. That was usually the way it worked on a game day, and today's game was pretty important. It was one-game elimination. If we lost, the season was over. If we won, we were in the finals next week.

Aaron gave me a slap on the back as he passed by, and Tammy offered me a smile. Apparently it was possible to have the whole family like me at the same time, although I really had no idea what their parents were thinking about me.

Junior handed me my bottle. "Donavan," he said.

I nodded. "Do you think he's sick?"

"Must be. I was hoping he'd play in the semi."

"Me too, but he still might be there for finals."

With the concussion protocols, he'd missed our last game and only been involved in noncontact drills at practices.

"Let's ask Coach," Junior suggested.

I wanted to know, but I was afraid of the answer. My stupid play had done this to Donavan. I'd hurt him, stopped him from playing and potentially hurt our chance to win it all.

Junior threw an arm around my shoulder. "It's not your fault," he said in my ear.

I wasn't surprised Junior knew what I was thinking. I would have been more surprised if he hadn't.

"Yeah, I guess," I agreed.

We all gathered around Coach.

"You've been working hard," he began. "I'm proud of you. Now most of you have noticed that Donavan wasn't at practice this morning."

We were going to get our question answered without our having to ask.

"Does that mean he's not going to be playing in today's game?" Junior asked.

"No. He won't be playing."

"Do you think he'll be back for the finals?" Junior questioned.

Coach took a deep breath. I held mine. "He won't be playing in the finals either."

I felt my whole body flush. This was all my fault. I was the one who'd injured him. He must still be hurting.

"I thought he was getting better," Aaron said.

"He's cleared to play," Coach replied.

"Then why won't he be?" Junior asked.

"Donavan is no longer a member of the team."

Everybody started talking.

Tammy broke through the noise. "Just because he was injured and missed some practices doesn't mean he should be kicked off! That's not fair!"

If anything, I was the one who should have been told to go.

"He hasn't been kicked off. In fact, I argued against this decision, but I couldn't convince them to allow Donavan to remain on the team."

"Convince them?" Junior said. "Who's them?"

Coach didn't answer immediately. It was clear he was struggling for words. "I'm afraid Ms. Jones has ordered that we not fully disclose the reasons—"

"Ms. Jones kicked him off the team?" Tammy cut him off.

"Of course not! Ms. Jones tried to convince Donavan's parents not to pull him from the team."

"Why would his parents do that?" Aaron asked.

"I'm sorry, but I can't discuss their reasons."

"Don't we deserve to know?" Tammy asked.

Coach nodded. "I agree, but I'm prohibited from sharing."

There was an outburst of discussion, with everybody talking to everybody else all at once.

"Quiet down. Let me finish," Coach said. "The important thing for us is to take care of the things we can take care of. We're still playing a game tonight. We need to stay focused, do our best and win that game."

"That one and the finals," Aaron said.

"And the finals. Okay, get changed and don't be late for class."

As everyone headed off toward the change rooms, Junior grabbed me by the arm. We waited until we were alone.

"We're the captains," Junior whispered. "Our team deserves answers, and we're going to get them."

"Mr. Tanner said he couldn't tell us anything else."

"He can't tell us, but I know who can."

Donavan gave us a weak little wave as we walked over. "You guys heard?"

"Yeah, Coach told us," Junior said.

"I'm sorry. I feel like I'm letting everyone down."

"You're a good player," Junior said.

"And our friend," I added.

Donavan looked really upset.

"Can you tell us what happened?" Junior asked.

"My mother happened."

"I don't understand."

Donavan slammed his locker closed.

"It's because of my mother. I don't think my father would have done it, but my mother convinced him. They went to Ms. Jones and Mr. Tanner and told them I was off the team."

"But why would they want you to quit?" I asked.

"It's because of everything that happened."

"I'm really sorry. I didn't mean to hurt you!" I said.

"If that's all that had happened, it wouldn't have been a problem."

I felt a sense of relief. It was good to know it wasn't all my fault.

"What else was she upset about?" Junior asked.

Donavan let out a big sigh. "Look, this is hard, and I don't agree, but she thought there were things that weren't what she called morally right."

"I don't know what that means," Junior said.

"She was upset about Aaron being punched and what happened between Jordan and him at the game."

"None of that was good," I admitted.

"We shouldn't have done those things," Junior said.

"She also didn't think Tammy should have been allowed to be part of the boys' team."

I didn't see that one coming.

"When she found out that Tammy was dating somebody on the team, she went on and on about what could have been happening in the change room."

"We have separate change rooms!" I argued.

"I told her, but it doesn't matter. She said she didn't like what she saw between the two of you at the dance."

"She saw them dancing and one kiss. Big deal!" Junior exclaimed.

"I told her the same thing. It was just a kiss. She told me that was proof that I was being led astray."

"That's ridiculous," Junior said. "Those are the reasons?"

"More or less." Donavan avoided looking at us as he said it.

"It sounds like there's more," Junior said. "What else is there?"

Donavan shrugged. "She doesn't like that some of the kids on the team come from broken homes."

"Broken?" Junior asked.

"It's not my word, it's hers. She believes that marriage is a death-'til-you-part sort of deal."

"About a quarter of the kids in the school live with one parent or the other or alternate back and forth," Junior said. "Lots of kids' parents aren't together."

"I know. That's only part of it."

"What's the rest?" I asked.

Donavan looked really uncomfortable. "You have to understand. It's not what I think. It's not me. Really."

"What's not you?"

"You know my father works at the plant."

"Lots of kids at our school have somebody that works there. So what?" Junior said.

"My father heard about your father," he said to me. "He told my mother. Then that email went home telling parents about the GSA. She wasn't too happy. I don't agree with her. I don't agree with any of it. It's not me." Donavan looked like he was on the verge of tears.

Junior put a hand on his shoulder. "We know it's not you, buddy."

"It's not. Honestly!"

"We believe you," I said.

"I better get to class. I'll see you guys at lunch. If it's okay, can I still sit with you?"

"Whether you play or not, you're still part of the team," Junior said.

"Thanks, guys." Donavan turned to walk off, then turned back. "Ryker?"

"Yeah?"

"Even my dad thinks your dad is kind of brave."

I didn't know what to say. "Thanks," I mumbled.

"Can you believe his parents did this to him?" I asked once Donavan had left.

"Can you imagine how bad it would be for Donavan if he came out? His mother would have a heart attack."

"I guess that's one way to get rid of her," I said. "But you don't think Donavan is gay, do you?"

"What if he was? He'd need the support of the GSA. He'd need support. Period." Junior turned to me. "Would he have yours?"

"Of course he would. Donavan's our friend."

"Good, because everyone needs support. Everyone."

I knew what Junior was saying. I had a flash of anger, followed immediately by sadness. My dad.

Junior must have read my face. "Exactly."

"It would make it easier for him." But I wasn't sure I could honestly say I wanted things easier for my dad. At least, not all the time. He'd still changed things on us, no matter the reasons, and my mom and I had been left to clean up the mess.

"And easier for you. Tammy might love a cause—"

"She does. Even she admits it."

"—but she still cares a lot about the world and everyone in it. That includes you," Junior said.

I didn't answer as I thought that over.

"At least one thing is clearer now," Junior continued.

"What's that?"

"Tammy is way too good for you."

"You're such a jerk."

"But a supportive jerk. Come on. We better get to class."

We started walking, and then Junior stopped and spun around so he was facing me.

"And the club is there for you and me too. That's all part of the alliance thing."

I didn't answer.

"Is everything okay?" Junior asked.

I shook my head. I wasn't sure how it could be when not only me but my entire family was the reason Donavan had been pulled from the team.

Twenty-Nine

The clock ticked down. The game would start in less than ten minutes. I walked over to the bench, took a sip of water and looked around. The bleachers were almost filled. That wasn't surprising, as even parents who didn't come to regular season games wanted to be there for the playoffs. What was surprising was that Donavan's dad was there. He hadn't shown up when Donavan was playing, and now he was there when his son wasn't playing.

Donavan sat on the edge of the stage, looking uncomfortable. Behind him the bake sale fundraiser was going on. The smell of all those goodies filled the gym, covering up the usual lingering odors of sweat and sanitizing cleaners.

My mother and a bunch of other parents, including Junior's and Donavan's mothers, were selling cupcakes and other assorted treats that would help buy new sports equipment and uniforms for the school teams. There was a steady lineup on the stage and stretching down the stairs of people waiting to buy. The game aside, the bake sale was already a big winner. It always was.

Unfortunately, my dad's baking wasn't part of the sale. He was supposed to make something, but there had been some big problems at the plant and he'd been called in early again.

I looked to the spot where he usually stood. It was empty. Whatever the problem was, it was big enough to keep him away. My body involuntarily shivered. He'd always been there. Even that had changed now.

Junior grabbed his water bottle. "Nice turnout," he said. "Including your own personal social worker."

Mrs. Mercer was sitting with Ms. Jones halfway up the stands.

"I hope we can give them something to cheer about. Or at least something we can talk about in our next meeting," I said.

Junior went to answer when a scream came from the far end of the gym. Angelique and three of her friends were holding large hand-drawn signs and jumping up and down. She'd made a point of telling me they were going to be there, but this kind of support was embarrassing. The sign she was holding read *We love you Jordie!* except *love* was a heart and so was the dot over the *i* in my name. She'd told me she was going to ask for permission to set up a Pep Club to cheer on the school teams and that Tammy wasn't the only girl who could set up a club. She'd told me she hoped I'd come watch when the girls' team played.

"Must be nice to have a fan club."

"They're here for the team."

"I don't see my name on any of those signs," Junior said. "That girl is putting a full-court press on you. Who knows? This might help you get back together with Tammy."

"How do you figure?"

Before he could answer, Tammy came over. She looked at the four girls jumping up and down.

"Some people make the team, and others just cheer for them," she said.

I thought better of mentioning that Angelique had made the girls' team.

"Hey, don't knock cheerleading," Junior said. "Those people are real athletes."

"Those four?" Tammy asked.

"Well. Not them. Real cheerleaders," Junior replied.

Tammy laughed. "They're just here to look good."

"What's wrong with looking good?" Junior asked.

"The way they're acting is so obvious. It's pathetic and embarrassing," she said, ignoring Junior. "Don't you think, Jordan?"

"I guess. Speaking of embarrassing, I wonder how Donavan's doing."

We turned away from Angelique and her crew.

"He must be feeling pretty lousy," Junior said.

"His mother has been giving me dirty looks," Tammy commented. "But that's nothing compared to how she's looking at your mothers."

"What do you mean?" I asked.

"Haven't you noticed? It's not just us. It's your mother

and Junior's too. I'm kind of glad my mom isn't here," Tammy said.

"Have you noticed any of that, Junior?' I asked.

"Yeah—at least, her giving me dirty looks. I flash her a big smile whenever she does," Junior said. "Kill 'em with kindness is my motto. I got an idea. Follow me."

He started walking toward the stage, and I grabbed him by the arm.

"Is this going to get us in trouble?"

"No trouble. Just spreading a little love."

He walked over to where Donavan was sitting.

"We didn't expect to see you here," Junior said to him.

"It's okay. Right?"

"As far as we're concerned, you're still on the team, so this is where you should be. Nothing's changed from earlier." Junior reached up and gave Donavan a fist bump.

"Great to see you, Donavan!" Tammy yelled loudly as she bumped fists with him too.

I looked past them to Donavan's mother. Her expression was like she'd bitten down on something sour. There was only one thing I could do. It was my turn. Donavan and I exchanged a very big, very loud, high five.

The buzzer sounded. I jumped. Time to start. We trotted over to the bench, where Coach was waiting.

"I'll keep this brief, people," he said.

I looked over at Tammy. She knew why. It had taken most of the season, but she'd trained Coach to finally stop using the word *guys*.

"This is a make-or-break game. I want all of you playing a game we can be proud of. A clean game." He looked directly at me, then Junior, then Aaron. "If I see or hear anything even remotely concerning out there, I've been instructed by Ms. Jones to forfeit. Do we all understand?"

There were nodding heads and mumbled agreements.

"We can do this. Now get out there, loosen up, and let's have fun."

Tammy tossed a ball over her shoulder at me. I didn't expect it but caught it at the last second.

"You heard Coach," she said. "Make us proud, Ryker. Or do you prefer I say, *Jordie, I heart you*?"

At halftime we had a huge lead. The other team was having an off night, fumbling the ball, making bad calls. We were in a groove. Coach put Tammy in Donavan's normal starting position, and the team seemed to rally, the chemistry was good, and every mistake the other team made, we took possession and scored.

"We're going to start the second half with our starters on the bench," Coach said.

"Shouldn't we stay in at least for the first part of the quarter?" Aaron asked.

"I'm going to throw in the younger players. They'll be the starters next year. It's good for them to know how it feels to be on the court during a playoff game. Besides, we want to win, not humiliate the other team."

"They should feel humiliated," Aaron said. "My baby sister is beating them, and we haven't played better all season. I say we continue to go at them hard. No mercy."

"Aaron, did I miss something?" Coach asked. "Did somebody promote you from co-captain to coach when I wasn't looking?"

There were comments from players. Coach held up his hand to silence everyone.

"We want a clean game. We don't need to demoralize anyone. If they close the lead too much, you guys—you people will be well-rested and ready to bring it home."

Coach named off the players who were going to start the half. The rest of us sat down on the bench. Tammy sat right beside me.

Angelique and the other girls started jumping up and down, waving their signs and screaming again. They ran along the sidelines, trying to get the crowd hyped.

At that moment Ms. Jones came down from the bleachers and walked over to where they were cheering. They talked briefly, and then she walked to the far end of the gym. The girls followed behind. They gathered around her in the far corner as play began in the second half. I was more interested in what was going on over there than on the court. One by one the girls handed Ms. Jones the signs and walked, heads down, back to the bleachers to sit.

Tammy laughed. "That was my favorite play of the entire game."

There was another cheer as our opponents scored

a basket. I turned back to the game taking place on the court.

There was less than three minutes to go. The other team had closed the gap, but it had never gotten close enough to our score for Coach to consider putting us back in. I had never spent so much time on the bench in my life. It meant I had a lot of time to watch the game as well as what was going on around it.

Just after the start of the fourth quarter, my dad had appeared in his usual spot. I was glad he was there but sorry he hadn't gotten to see me play. Whatever was happening at the plant had to be pretty serious, but I was sure he'd sorted it out. That's what he did. At least at work. I wished he could have sorted out everything else as easily.

Angelique and the girls had stayed in their seats the whole half, although she had waved at me a few times, trying to get my attention. A couple of times I'd given her a little return wave, hoping Tammy wouldn't notice. I wouldn't admit it out loud, but it was nice to have somebody doing that for me.

My mom had disappeared from the stage. There were still some parents standing behind the tables selling things, but she wasn't one of them. It felt like I'd spent more time scanning the gym, trying to figure out where she'd gone, than I had watching the actual game. But she wasn't anywhere I could see. She wouldn't have left. I considered asking for permission to leave the bench to find her, but that wouldn't have looked good.

I turned my attention back to the game. The clock, mercifully, was ticking down to almost nothing. The buzzer sounded. It was over. We were in the finals.

I was the first dressed and out of the change room again. I really wanted to find Mom and talk to Dad. Standing just outside the door was Angelique. She gave me a smile.

"Sorry we couldn't cheer more. Ms. Jones took away our signs."

"I saw."

"She said we couldn't act like a club until we have permission."

"That makes sense. I need to go find my parents."

"I saw them. They're down toward the back doors. Your mother seemed really upset."

"I have to go." I didn't need a scene at school.

Angelique looked hurt.

"Thanks for the sign. It was nice," I said. "See you Monday."

She perked up and did a too-big smile that reminded me of my mom.

"Definitely," she said. "Unless you want to play ball over the weekend."

"Thanks for the offer, but I'm not sure about this weekend. You know...family stuff."

I turned the corner and saw my parents way down the corridor. My dad had his arms around my mom. I rushed over. Mom looked like she had been crying.

"What's wrong? What did you do?" I demanded of him.

He looked shocked and hurt.

"He didn't do anything," my mom said. "Please, let's go."

We walked out the side door, circled around the school and headed for the almost-emptied parking lot. The only cars left belonged to parents still waiting for a player. The Camaro was parked in the far corner. We went to my mom's truck.

"Is somebody going to tell me what happened?" I asked.

"It's nothing," she said, but she looked like she was going to start crying again.

"If it was nothing, you wouldn't be like this."

"Some things were said to your mother," my dad said.

"What sort of things?"

There was a pause before he answered. "Things about me, about our family."

I felt a flush of anger. "Who?"

"People we thought were our friends," my dad said. "I'll take care of it. You and your mother get home."

Dad practically guided her into the truck. I climbed in beside her. He leaned in the window.

"Mandy, are you going to be all right?" he asked her.

"I'll be fine to drive."

"I didn't mean that."

"I'll be fine. Thanks, Chris."

"Jordan, take care of her."

I nodded.

She turned the key. The engine growled but didn't catch. She tried again. It wouldn't turn over.

"It sounds like the starter," my dad said.

"It hasn't been starting so easily the last couple of days," she replied.

"Pop the hood and give it another try."

He circled around to the front of the truck and opened the hood, blocking our view of him.

"What happened?" I asked.

"Just some ignorant people saying ignorant things."

"About Dad?"

"About your father, about our marriage, about me. It's been hard for me. It must be hard on you."

"It hasn't been easy. At least you didn't toss a basketball at somebody's head."

"That's only because I didn't have one," she said.

"I recommend it."

My mom snorted a little.

My dad slammed the hood shut and came back around to the driver's-side window. He pulled his keys out of his pocket. "It's definitely the starter. Take the Camaro."

"Really?"

"I'll get the truck towed and fixed. You get home."

"How will you get back? Brodie?"

I scowled a little at her saying my dad's boyfriend's name so easily.

Dad shook his head. "No. I'll figure it out. Don't worry."

"Are you sure?" she asked.

"I'm sure. Go."

"Thanks, Chris. Really, thank you."

"You shouldn't be thanking me for anything."

I silently agreed.

Thirty

Mom not only had to adjust all the mirrors but also yank the seat forward almost all the way.

"Do you even know how to handle this thing?" I asked as she checked her blind spots.

The Camaro jumped forward as my mom wheeled out of the parking lot. I turned in my seat and saw my dad with a funny expression on his face, hands on his hips.

It was too bad Junior wasn't with us. My mom pushed the Camaro more than my dad ever did. She took corners almost on rails, whipping around, and let the car muscle forward as soon as lights turned green. She started to smile a little as she drove.

"Is this why Dad never lets you drive the Camaro?"

"What? I could have driven the Camaro whenever I wanted. I love my truck."

"Yeah, right. But this is Dad's baby. He never let you drive it."

"I didn't drive it, but not because he didn't let me."

"Then why didn't you? You obviously know how to work it."

My mom screeched a little rounding a corner. She was quiet for an entire block.

"Because I never really needed to drive it," she said. "And because your dad does."

"I thought you didn't even like the Camaro."

My mom's smile slipped. "It was easier to be angry at a car."

We were quiet again.

"I know how angry you are at him," she said.

"Aren't you angry?"

"Sometimes. I'm trying hard not to be, but it isn't my being angry that's hard on him. He can handle my being mad. We've had too much practice at that. Your being angry at him, that's completely different. He doesn't know what to do. And I can see he's trying to do right by everyone lately."

I didn't have an answer to that, because even if he was trying, things kept happening that were directly because of him. Things like tonight. So I kept quiet.

"I'm not saying you shouldn't be upset at him. I'm saying it hurts him more than you know."

"We don't deserve to be the only ones hurting," I said.

"No," Mom agreed. "We don't. None of us do. Including your dad."

We didn't speak for the last few blocks home. Mom swung the car and positioned it to back in.

"Can you leave it at the end of the driveway?" I asked. "I won't have to get you to move it in the morning. Junior and I want to get some extra practice in."

Mom backed the car up just enough for the nose to clear the curb.

Thirty-One

"Shouldn't Junior be here by now?" my mom asked, putting her morning coffee down and looking at the clock on the microwave. "Maybe you should text him. Or I could call his mom."

"She's at work. He'll be here any minute," I said. "Relax."

Mom lifted a spoonful of sugary cereal to her mouth. "Your dad should have arrived too. He sent a message. The truck is back in working order. He got a secondhand starter from the wrecker and installed it. Let's go out to the porch and wait." She put her bowl into the sink.

As my mom opened the door, she stopped. I looked over her shoulder and saw my dad and Junior standing at the end of the driveway. Junior's bike was on its side in the road. Why were they waiting down there, I wondered.

I could see my dad talking to Junior. There was something about the way they were standing, staring at the car, that seemed serious. Mom noticed it too.

"Chris?" she called out, and he turned toward us. He looked upset. In bare feet, she started walking down the driveway. I stooped to put on my basketball shoes. I didn't tie them up. She stopped a few feet away from the Camaro. I wasn't there yet when I heard her swear. I was shocked. I'd never heard her swear before, not even when she and my dad had fought at their worst.

"Who would do this?" she demanded.

My dad shook his head. I moved around my mom and stopped.

We all stared down at the Camaro. Jagged gouges in the paint, silver against the yellow and black of the hood, stood out in the morning light.

"I found it like this," Junior said. "With *that* written on it. Mr. R, I'm so sorry."

The letters stared up at us.

My dad's head hung. He reached out a hand to touch the hood of the car and traced the jags nearest him with his fingers.

"They didn't just key it," he said. "It's scraped in. It's down to the metal."

My mom moved beside my dad. She took his arm. He turned in to her and bent down, folding his body against hers. She wrapped her arms around him and patted his back.

"I'm so sorry, Chris," she said. "I know what this car means to you. I should have never left it down here. This is my fault."

"It's not your fault," my dad mumbled against her.

Except I'd asked for the car to be left at the end of the driveway. I could have told my mom to park it in the garage. Something went solid in my stomach.

"Why would someone do this?" Dad asked.

Mom hushed him. "We'll get it fixed. It can be fixed."

My dad straightened and sniffed as he wiped the back of his hand across his nose. "It happened in our own driveway."

"Come inside, Chris. I've got a pot of coffee. We'll figure this out. You two boys will be okay, right?"

"Sure, Mrs. R. We'll be fine."

My mom led my dad by the arm past the Camaro.

"It's only a car," I said. It must have sounded meaner than I meant it to. But it was just a car. Just a thing.

My dad stopped and looked back at me. Tears inched down his cheeks. He shook his head as my mom continued to take him inside.

"Why did you say that?" Junior asked.

"Because it's true," I said. I pointed at the hood. "And so is that."

Junior stared down at where I was pointing. Then he stared at me.

"It's not true like that," he said. "Not the way the person who scraped that in meant it."

I didn't answer. The gouges ran deep. The car was scarred now. It would be a big job to fix it, but he'd fixed the old thing before. He could fix it again.

"He'll repair it," I said.

Junior shook his head. "You can fix the car, but you can't just fix something like this. This is more than scraped paint. This is a personal attack."

"My dad can't just expect everyone to be okay with what he did."

"He shouldn't expect someone to write that into the hood of his car either," Junior responded quickly.

I rolled my eyes and felt a little queasy. "All I hear about is how hard stuff must be for my dad and how he needs support and understanding."

"He does!"

"And I'm tired of you always being on his side no matter what. It's like you have some sort of crush on him."

Junior looked like I'd hit him. "If I had a dad like yours—"

"But you don't! You get to have a dead dad who can do no wrong!"

From the expression on Junior's face, I knew I'd crossed the line. I knew I'd hit below the belt. And I didn't care. I was tired of everyone defending my dad just because he'd come out, like he was some sort of hero or deserved some sort of sympathy. Everything crappy that had happened to me and my mom was a consequence of his walking out on us. I didn't know why no one else wanted to see it when it was so clear.

I knew I should apologize to Junior. Instead I crossed my arms over my chest.

"Is that really how you see this?" Junior finally asked. "That you'd rather have a dead dad than a gay one?"

That wasn't what I had meant, but I wasn't willing to give way to Junior. I shrugged.

"You really don't get it," Junior said.

"I'm tired of people telling me what I don't get. I get a lot."

"You don't get enough." Junior looked down at the car's hood. Then he stared directly in my eyes and wouldn't look away. "You don't get me either. That's an attack on your father, on you! It's an attack on me," Junior said more quietly. "I'm that too, Jay. I'm one of those. Now what?"

We stared at each other.

If he meant what I thought he was saying, it just couldn't be true. Junior was smooth with the girls, probably the most popular kid in our grade and maybe even the school, funny, a great point guard, the friend I'd known forever. My *best* friend. The person I knew best in the world outside of my mother and my…father.

Finally I said, "Quit kidding around."

"I'm not kidding anyone about anything. I'm gay." Junior looked away and picked up his bike. "You don't deserve a father like yours, and he doesn't deserve to be treated like this. Neither do I. No one deserves to see that written about them."

The silver glistening up from the hood was an accusation.

"Junior—" I began.

"At least I know what not to expect from you now," Junior said as he stood on the pedals of his bike and pushed off in a hard turn toward me. "You won't stand by your own dad. I shouldn't have thought you'd stand by me."

I had to take one step back as he pedaled off.

I kicked the front fender of the Camaro, but it didn't budge.

Thirty-Two

I slammed the front door as I went inside. I went through the house and found them sitting together at the kitchen table. A bunch of papers was spread out in front of them, and the cordless phone was on the table beside them.

My mom saw me and began to gather the papers together.

"Where's Junior?" my dad asked.

"He had to go home," I lied, quickly and easily. I didn't want to talk about how my dad had caused another fight between my best friend and me. I definitely didn't want to tell my parents what Junior had told me. Part of me didn't want to get into it. Part of me knew it was because it wasn't mine to share. How would I even tell them? "We're going to catch up later."

The phone rang, and my mom jumped. She picked it up on the second ring.

"Hi. Yes," she said. "Right, we'd appreciate it. Forty minutes. Yes, thank you."

She put the phone back down.

I had the terrible thought that it was Junior's mom phoning to complain about me.

"Who was that?" I asked.

"That was the police. I phoned to report what happened to your father's car. They're sending over somebody to take a report."

I let out a sigh of relief. I sat down and looked at the papers on the table. There was a real estate ad. I held the pamphlet up.

"Are you moving out of your place?" I asked my dad.

He and my mom exchanged a look.

"I'm not moving," Dad said.

"If it's not you..." It dawned on me. "Are we selling the house?"

"I thought it was a good idea to get some numbers," my mom began.

"We're selling the house?" I asked again.

"Why don't you sit down," my dad suggested.

"Figures," I muttered.

"What was that?"

"Figures," I said louder. "I'm the last one around here to be told anything. When were you planning to break the news, when the moving truck showed up?"

"Jordie, we haven't decided anything," my mom said. "We're seeing what our options are."

"But no decisions have been made, and they wouldn't be without you," my dad said.

"Are we that bad off?"

"There's a lot of factors," my dad said.

"Right. Aren't there always?"

"What does that mean?"

"It means there's always a lot of reasons and a lot of factors. And they always lead back to one thing, Dad!"

"Jordie, we're not moving. Like I said, we're looking at options. Right now, though, there's something more important we have to deal with." She moved to stand beside my father. "I called the police because what happened on the driveway was a hate crime."

"You mean on our soon-to-be-ex-driveway in front of our soon-to-be-ex-home." I turned on my dad. "I'm tired of you ruining my life. There's not one part of it you haven't messed up."

My dad's shoulders sank. "Is that how you really feel?"

"My family is gone. My girlfriend is gone. I'm in counseling so that basketball won't be gone. And now my home is on the way out too. It's your fault!"

His shoulders dropped a little more. "You're right," he said. "He's right," he repeated to my mom.

"Chris," she said.

"He's right. I thought I was making my life right, not making everybody else's life wrong."

"That's not how it is," Mom said.

My dad gently pulled his arm out of her grasp. "You shouldn't be so nice to me."

"Maybe not," she said, taking his arm back and stroking it.

"You've got to be kidding!" I yelled at them. "You break up and you two are better together than ever? Where was this when you two were fighting all the time?"

"Jordie!" my mom snapped. "You need to walk away before you say anything else that you're going to regret. Go out and cool off. Maybe go over to Junior's place. Come back when you're calm enough to talk things out."

"No problem!" I ran from the room and out through the garage. I grabbed my bike and sailed down the driveway. They didn't bother to tell me things. I wasn't going to bother to tell them I wouldn't be going anywhere near Junior's. I didn't want to be around him any more than I wanted to be around them.

I pedaled hard up the hill, away from my house and parents. I stood on the pedals, hunched over the handlebars, my shoulders bobbing one at a time until I got to Ridge Town. My hair stuck to my forehead, and I could feel sweat beading up and pooling before it dribbled down the small of my back. I stopped when I could see Tammy's house. I was two doors down, across the street. I stood there panting.

If I went up to the house and rang the bell, then what? Would I tell Tammy why I was standing at her front door again? Would I tell her it wasn't just because I wanted to get back together? Would she understand? Would she want to be with me even though she was the type of girl who started a GSA and I was the type of guy who blamed his dad for someone wrecking his car? And who had just told his best friend he should be glad his father had died? I couldn't imagine that Tammy, with her backpack of buttons and her causes and her full-body smile that made me tongue-tied, would want to be with that guy.

So I stared at her house and didn't move. I imagined her family inside, muffins baking in the oven, Tammy and her mom at the table, working on laptops, while Aaron and his dad played video games in the next room.

I imagined my mom comforting my dad, and him calling his behemoth boyfriend, both of them telling my father everything would be fine. I was nowhere in the mix. They didn't even know where I was. And no one was telling me anything would be fine.

I exhaled as I gave Tammy's house one last look. Junior was right. Tammy deserved a better guy.

I pushed off and pedaled past her house. I kept going, leaving Ridge Town but not really sure what direction I should take. Anywhere but home would do. It seemed like maybe I wouldn't have any type of home soon anyway.

Thirty-Three

If I'd known I was going to be gone all day and into the evening, I would have at least brought more money with me. Around lunchtime I stopped at a coffee shop and bought a sandwich. I didn't have quite enough for it, but the woman behind the counter said not to worry when I apologized. She made up the difference out of the tip jar. I thanked her and left, riding my bike until I found a playground I'd never been to before. I stopped to eat on a bench.

The sandwich was dry. I wished I had a drink, but I'd had no money to buy one. I didn't see a fountain anywhere in the playground. I chewed each bite an extra long time. I sat there until the sun slanted harshly and I had to squint. I knew it would set before too long. I got back onto my bike and figured I had nowhere left to go but home, so I turned around.

I thought I passed the coffee shop again, but the neighborhood looked different. The buildings were a different color of brick. I turned my bike around and tried to retrace my path to the playground. I never found it.

I circled around. I tried to find a familiar street name, and when I couldn't, I thought maybe I should keep going on streets with names I didn't recognize until I ended up back somewhere I knew. When that didn't help, I looked at the sun and tried to figure out the right direction by that.

There was only one choice—and I didn't want to make it. I didn't want to call my mom and ask for help. I didn't even want to talk to her, but what else could I do? I stopped and took out my phone, expecting to see a hundred messages from my parents, wondering where I was. Instead all I saw was a black screen. I held the power button, and the phone flashed the No Battery sign.

I was too tired to ride my bike anymore, so I decided to walk away from the sun and just hope for the best. The buildings here looked like abandoned warehouses. There weren't any stores to go into or houses to go up to. Not that knocking on a stranger's door and going into their house to use their phone would be smart anyway. I knew that.

I sat down on the curb and vowed that in five minutes I'd get up again. I'm sure I sat there longer than five minutes. My legs still hurt. I realized it wasn't just my legs that hurt. There was a tightness in my chest, and my legs felt dead under the pain. I could hear my dad telling me that even if it was the last two minutes of the game and we were down by twenty, to play like I always did. So I got up and began walking my bike again.

I heard a vehicle pull over across from me, and a door open. I looked over my shoulder and saw a nosebleed-red truck and the giant who drove it. I kept walking.

"Jordan!" he called from across the street as he lumbered after me.

I stopped but didn't look back at him.

"Jordan!" he boomed again.

I stretched my neck and tilted my head back, closing my eyes. *Anyone but Brodie. Anyone.*

"Where are you going?" he asked.

"Home," I answered, without opening my eyes.

"It's a long walk. Let me give you a ride."

"I'm good," I said, opening my eyes and continuing to walk.

Brodie pulled out his keys and pressed a button. His truck's headlights flashed and the horn beeped. "If you won't take a ride, then we're walking."

"I'm walking. Alone," I corrected him.

He continued to walk after me.

"Alone," I repeated. "I don't want to see my dad's boyfriend. Not today."

"Then don't look," Brodie said. "But I'm not his boyfriend anymore."

I was curious, even though I really didn't want to talk to him.

Brodie shadowed me. I stopped. Brodie stopped. I took a few more steps. So did Brodie.

"This is creepy, dude," I said.

"This is a public sidewalk, *dude*," Brodie answered. "I'm not letting some kid walk through this neighborhood at this time of day by himself. Your choice. A truck ride or a long walk, but both are going to be with me."

I huffed. "Whatever," I said as I turned the bike around.

Brodie unlocked his truck with the key fob but had to go behind it to unlock the tailgate manually. He lifted my bike into the back of the truck with one hand, placing it among a bunch of coolers.

"Want to call one of your folks?" he asked.

I held up my phone. "Dead."

He offered me his, but I didn't reach out to take it.

"One of us has to call. Me or you?"

"Not me."

He shrugged. He pushed a button on the screen of his phone. I heard it ringing.

"Hey, Chris, it's me. I found him. He's fine. He's right here beside me. I'm bringing him back now. I've got to drop something off at the shop first. We'll be there soon." Brodie ended the call.

"Climb in," he said to me.

I opened the door and had to reach for a grip to pull myself into the cab. The interior was all black leather with red topstitching and chrome detailing that matched the exterior. Brodie's elbows hit against his door and rested on the center console. The truck still had that new-car smell.

"Buckle up."

That was the only thing said until we reached Brodie's store. He swung the truck around back and stopped in front of a fenced-off area. Taking the keys from the ignition, he jumped out of the truck, undid a chain on the fence and pushed open the gates before driving us inside.

"Let's go. I can't let good product spoil," he said as he swung out of the truck again. He opened the tailgate and pulled two coolers toward him, stacking them before he lifted them, and walked toward a steel door in the wall. He sandwiched the coolers between his hip and the bricks as he unlocked the door and went in. I followed him.

The back of Brodie's shop was almost all stainless steel. There were all sorts of knives hanging off magnetic strips. There was a gigantic walk-in fridge at one end. He put the two plastic coolers down on the floor, opened the big metal door of the fridge and put the coolers inside. He quickly reappeared. The door closed with a loud thud.

"Health regulations. Had to get the meat refrigerated or I won't be able to sell it."

"Don't you get deliveries?" I asked.

"Not wild game." He went to a big stainless steel double sink, pushed up the sleeves of his sweater and took off his leather cuffs to wash his hands. "Let's get you home." He wiped his hands dry and slid his sleeves back down.

I followed him out again. He locked up and we got back into the truck. We drove out of the fenced area. He locked the gates once more and we were off.

"You're not going to try to ask me where I was or how I got there?"

"Nope," he answered.

"Were you looking for me?"

"Lots of people were looking for you. Your parents called everybody they knew. Lots of people were out trying to find you."

"I wasn't lost."

"Gotcha."

"Not at first anyway. I just needed to get away."

"You had your parents really worried. When your dad called, he was panicking."

"Why'd you even come looking for me if you're not his boyfriend anymore?"

"He's still a friend. I still care about him."

"Then why aren't you two together?" I asked before I had time to think better of it.

"I thought you wouldn't care."

"I didn't say I cared. I wanted to know why."

"Are you sure you really want to know?" Brodie asked in his deep voice.

I didn't answer. I was almost grateful he didn't push. Why did I want to know any of this?

Brodie finally said, "Your father is a good person, but he doesn't need a boyfriend. He doesn't know how to be a gay man, let alone another guy's boyfriend. He hasn't learned yet, and I can't be the one to teach him. He needs to figure that out on his own. Besides, he doesn't have the time even if I could show him."

"Because of the plant."

"Because of you," Brodie said. "His top priority is you. Not that that's wrong or I'm blaming either of you."

I thought of the mornings waking up without my dad and the smell of his cooking in the house, the bake sale he didn't deliver on, the basketball games he missed, all the problems he'd caused in my life. And I knew I blamed him.

"No proud man like your father phones the guy who dumped him unless it's really important. You're the most important thing in the world to him. That's as it should be."

"So you just helped him when he asked?"

"Sure. Didn't need to think twice about it."

"But why?"

"Because he's a good man with a good son."

"It's that simple?" I asked.

"Can't it be?"

I let out a big sigh. "Lately nothing has been simple. Everything is complicated. Everything is some big, complex issue."

I waited for a response but didn't get one, so I asked, "No lecture?"

Brodie shook his head. "Not my place."

I glanced over at him. His sleeves were pushed up a bit, and I could see something catching the light on his wrist. They were lines that looked to be a whiter white.

"What are those?" I pointed.

Brodie looked down, confused. Then, without saying a word, he pulled the truck over to the side of the road and came to a stop.

He turned on the interior lights of the cab and really pushed up both sleeves of his sweater. What was I supposed to see, that he had big muscles or—then I saw more clearly. They were raised white lines, paler than the skin around them and without freckles, up the inside of both his arms. His blue veins wove around and disappeared under them.

"These are my complicated."

"Did it happen at your store? Like, an accident?" I asked.

"These weren't an accident. They were self-inflicted. I did them when I probably wasn't much older than you."

I shuddered at the thought. "Why would you do that?"

"I didn't like who I was very much then, and I caused myself pain on the outside to try to take away the pain I was feeling inside. These lines remind me of what I felt like back then, when causing my own destruction was better than a reality I couldn't change. Probably a little of what your father must feel sometimes. Like, maybe, what you do too."

He loomed like a mountain, red, bushy beard, thick arms, wide shoulders. His scars were bold and obvious. How bad had those cuts been? How deep? I looked closer and noticed thinner, more delicate lines revealing themselves around the thick jags, momentary and fragile before they disappeared into freckled skin and red hair.

Brodie slid his sleeves back down. He no longer looked like some hulking mass, some huge, untouchable man.

"They're proof that we can survive even when we try to stop ourselves. I survived. You're going to survive all of this too, and then whatever else life throws your way. You figure out who you can rely on and you push forward, owning the things you did."

Who was it that I could rely on? Who was I supposed to turn to? Mrs. Mercer, who had been appointed? My dad? Junior? My mom, who was considering selling the house and moving us away? I didn't think I could count on Tammy, who even the whales could count on. And I couldn't blame my dad for any of that. Not when I'd been the one disappointing people and shoving them away, letting them down. My dad hadn't made me do those things. I'd done them.

"I've said some things," I said. "And done some things. Things that weren't good. That hurt people."

"Because you got hurt too, first by your dad leaving and then by the reason he had to leave."

I nodded ever so slightly. I looked at Brodie and for a second thought maybe there was something to this man. Maybe Brodie understood what I was going through. He wasn't telling me to be more sympathetic or understanding. It wasn't that he was being easy on me, but maybe my dad's ex-boyfriend was the only one who really got it.

"When you're hurt, the natural instinct is to hurt back. That doesn't make it right. But it does make you human. Making mistakes is human, but trying to make things right after makes you a better one."

"You make it sound simple," I said. "Easy."

He turned slightly to look at me. "Not easy, but yeah, as simple as that."

Thirty-Four

After we started driving again, Brodie put on the sound system and let me tune to whatever station I wanted on his satellite radio. I figured he did that because he didn't want any more silence but also because right then neither of us needed any more words. We pulled up in front of my house and parked.

My parents came out onto the porch.

"You good?" Brodie asked.

I didn't know if I was, but I nodded and reached for the door handle. Then I stopped.

"Brodie?"

"Mm-hmm?"

"You said my dad's a good guy."

"I did." He gripped the steering wheel. It looked like a toy in his hands.

"Then maybe you shouldn't have broken up with him."

Brodie laughed. It filled up the cab and wrapped around us. "I didn't expect to hear you say that."

"I didn't expect to say it." I paused. "Things that are wrong can be fixed. Simple as that."

"Really?"

"I heard some guy say that. I sort of believe him."

"I'm normally the one giving advice," he said.

"I'm normally the one ignoring it. At least get out of the truck for a minute. My dad—both my parents—will want to thank you."

Brodie shook his head, still smiling. "Only for a minute," he agreed. "I don't want to intrude where I'm not invited."

"I just invited you, dude."

"Right, *dude*."

I climbed out of the truck and started up the driveway. I deliberately walked on the driver's side of my dad's car. I didn't want to see that word. I didn't want Brodie to see it either as he trailed several feet behind me. There was already too much to explain, even though I suspected Brodie might have heard about the Camaro already.

My mom ran off the porch. Dad rushed after her. She threw her arms around me, and I threw my arms around her.

"I'm not sure whether to hug you or hit you," she whispered in my ear. "You scared me so badly."

"I'm sorry."

"You scared us both," Dad said as he hovered over us.

"I didn't mean to scare either of you. I'm sorry, Dad. I'm sorry for everything."

He reached out tentatively and put a hand on my shoulder. I threw an arm around him, and then he wrapped his arms around both of us. I knew I wasn't the only one fighting hard not to cry.

"Thank you for bringing him back," Mom said.

"Yes, thanks." My dad looked from me to Brodie.

"Just glad I ran into him. Don't be too hard on him. It's been pretty confusing for everybody. He's a good kid."

"No," my dad said. "He's the best kid."

I felt a flutter go through my entire body.

"Jordan's bike is in the back of my truck. I'll grab it."

"Help him, Chris." Mom gave my dad a small push.

They walked down the driveway. My mom and I watched, one of her arms still around me. Brodie pulled the bike out and handed it to my dad. He put it down. They stood, Brodie shifting from foot to foot. Then, although we were too far away to hear, they started talking.

"You're okay, right?" my mom asked.

"I'm okay—at least, I'm getting there."

"You know your dad loves you so much."

"I know."

We watched Brodie gesturing to the truck. My dad shook his head. Brodie nodded as my dad talked.

"He told me he wished he'd never told anybody," my mom said. "He didn't realize how much he'd hurt us."

"I'm kind of glad he did."

"Really?" She sounded surprised.

"Maybe not glad exactly. But he needed to. I understand that now, or at least a little more than I did."

My dad came back up the driveway with my bike, smiling

to himself. Brodie tapped the horn and waved as he drove away. My parents both waved back.

"We need to talk," Mom said. "But first you need to get warmed up, get a hot drink into you and something to eat. I'll fix something. For all of us."

I took another long sip of cocoa. It was my third cup, and I'd also eaten two gigantic bowls of mac and cheese. I hadn't realized how cold and hungry and empty I'd been.

"Do you want something else?" my mom asked.

"I'm fine. Thanks, Mom."

"Good. Chris, another coffee?"

"Thanks. I'll get it."

He got up and helped himself before he sat down again.

"First off, you have to know that I'd never—*we'd* never—sell the house without you being part of the discussion," my mom said.

"We were just talking about possibilities," Dad added.

"I know things are tough with money. If we have to move, then we have to move." I clinked my spoon against the empty bowl.

"They're not that tough. We can get by, especially now, because of your dad. He has a solution."

I looked at him.

"I'm going to get the car fixed and —"

"I'm sorry for what I said. I know it's more than a car."

"It *is* more than a car. That's why I'm going to sell it."

"You're selling it?" I couldn't believe what he was saying. My dad loved the Camaro. It was a classic, his baby, his father's. It wasn't *just* a car. Even my mom knew it.

"There are always people interested in buying it. Finding a buyer will be easy. I know I can get close to $100,000 for it."

"You can't do that. We'll move. We can sell the house. It's okay. You can't do that for me."

"I'm not doing it for you. At least, not *just* for you. It's for all of us. It's for me."

"I don't understand. That car means everything to you."

"Not as much as I thought and not the way that I thought. It isn't even my car. It's my father's. It's time to let go of that past. The anger, the hurt, the things I can never do to make him happy or that I can never fix between him and me. It's more important that I fix things between the two of us." He looked at my mom. "And try to fix them between you and me as well, Mandy."

My mom sipped her coffee, then said, "I'm surprised there's a you and me, but I'd like to try to fix things too."

"It's time to move forward instead of looking backward," he said. "That was what I was hoping for in all this. And it *is* just a car."

"I'm going to miss it," I said.

"So am I, but not as much as I miss some other things. I'm sorry for all the pain I've caused you. Caused both of you." He reached out and placed a hand on top of my mom's.

"You didn't cause all of it. I didn't always help," Mom said.

"I didn't either," I added.

"I hope we can work on some things that are a lot more important than some stupid car. Do you think we can do that? Or is that too simple?" he asked.

"Why can't it be as simple as fixing stuff up?" I thought about what else I needed to fix. "I need to go and see Junior."

"Now?" my mom asked. "It's almost nine thirty."

"Can't it wait until tomorrow?" my dad questioned. "I already let his mom know we found you."

That last part made me feel worse—and more determined to see Junior that night. "No, it can't. I need to talk to him. That is, if he'll agree to talk to me. Even if he won't, I still need to say some stuff to him tonight."

"It's that serious?" Mom asked.

"Yes."

"Do you want to tell us about it first?"

"No." It wasn't mine to tell. Not all of it anyway. The big part was Junior's, and I didn't have his permission to blab it.

"Was this something I caused too?" my dad asked.

"No. I was wrong to blame everything on you. I messed this one up all by myself."

"Tell you what. I'll call his mother and let her know it's important and that I'm driving you over," my dad said.

"I'll come too," Mom said. "We need to thank Junior and his mom for looking for you. You'll drive my truck, Chris."

Thirty-Five

I followed Junior into the backyard. He took a seat on one side of the picnic bench. I sat on the other side, the table stretching out between us. There wasn't much light except for the little halo thrown by the lamp over the back door of his house. It felt okay to be seated in the dark. We could see each other but not too clearly.

"Do your parents know why you're here?" Junior asked.

I was relieved that Junior had started. "They know we got into a fight. They know it was my fault."

"Do they know what I told you?"

"No. I didn't say anything about that."

"Because you didn't know what to say to them or because you're embarrassed or what?" Junior asked.

I thought for a minute. "Yes....and yes, I guess. I'm sorry—not embarrassed, but not knowing what to say. But there's more than that."

"What more?"

"It's up to you to tell people or not tell them. It's not for me to do it."

"At least you understand that," Junior said. He exhaled and seemed less tense.

"What did you tell your mother about my needing to come over to talk?"

"I told her we got into a fight because you'd been a jerk," he said.

"So you told her the truth."

Junior laughed nervously. That made me feel a tiny bit better.

"Seriously, I was a jerk. I could have acted better, and I didn't. I'm sorry."

"At least you understand that too," Junior said.

Junior's mom pulled aside the curtain on the back door and looked out at us before she let it drop.

"Does she know, you know, about you?" I asked.

He shook his head. "I've only told one person, and that didn't work out so well for me."

I sighed. I felt so bad.

"That was the first time I'd ever said those words out loud. I'd never even said them when I was alone and nobody could hear. That wasn't fair to just blab them out at you."

"No. I wasn't fair to you."

The picnic bench creaked.

"Were you surprised?" Junior asked.

"Shocked," I admitted.

"You had no idea? Never?"

"None. But I don't seem to be particularly good at figuring out these things. I lived with a gay guy my whole life and never suspected anything."

He laughed again, and this time it seemed to come more easily.

"Are you going to tell anyone else?" I asked.

"I'm not sure. I wasn't even planning on telling you. At least, not yet. It just happened. I said it before I thought about it."

"I'm happy you did."

"You are?" he asked.

"Definitely. I didn't show it. I'm sorry about that. It wasn't what I expected, and then I screwed up and made it about me and how I felt, and I never stopped to think about you. Not really."

"But it isn't about you," Junior said.

"I know. But for those seconds it was like, I'm the guy with a gay father *and* a gay best friend. What does that say about me? What would everyone think of me?"

"Did you ever think no one would think about you at all? Did you think maybe they'll see you as someone's son and someone's friend?"

"I am someone's son. We're still friends, right?"

"Haven't we had this discussion before? You're my best friend. That hasn't changed for me."

"Me neither," I said.

"Some things don't change," Junior said. "You're still slow on the pickup. You better work on that before the big game."

The picnic bench creaked as we got up. He stopped before we went inside.

"When I do decide to tell people, it might be hard."

"If anybody wants to take you on, they'll have to go through me."

"No," Junior replied. "I'll have to deal with it. I know you'll be here to be a support and you're going to have my back, but I need to handle things myself, in my own way."

"I'll be there for you whenever and however you decide. I'll be your own personal gay-straight alliance."

Junior turned to face me. "I don't know how to do this. How to be this. What if I mess it up?"

"Then you're human, and you try to fix things, and you ask your best friend what to do because he's had lots of practice messing things up."

"It will be hard on you. People will say stuff about your best friend being gay. About you being gay."

"I get that it might be crappy, but it's just words. You have to try to ignore them."

"But—"

"I know it may hurt and suck. It may also be better in ways you didn't think."

"Like?"

"Like I might actually like my dad's boyfriend. I mean, if they work it out. I hope they do."

I could see Junior's eyes get wide even in the little light there was. "For serious?"

I nodded. "And there may be an upside to all this for me."

"And that would be?" Junior asked.

"All those girls who have crushes on you will be upset. They might need a shoulder to cry on." I dusted off my shoulder the way Junior would have, dressed in his Sunday best. "Isn't that what gay best friends do? Help fix up their straight friends?"

Junior shook his head and laughed. "Some stuff doesn't change. You're still dense. You know, Jay, in a bizarre sort of way, I'm proud of you for thinking that way. Although Tammy might be jealous of the other girls."

"I think we both realized she's too good for me."

He put an arm around my shoulder. "Maybe not anymore. You're kind of improving. A work in progress. You should talk to her. Actually talk to her."

"I don't think there's a point. It's over."

"Maybe that is the point. If it's really over, you can both move forward."

I thought about how much moving forward had happened tonight already. Or had begun to. I didn't want to hurt anymore. I didn't want anyone around me to either. That was really clear now.

"You know my mom had a biko in the oven."

Golden rice cake—it was one of my favorites. "I thought I smelled it when we came in."

"It should be out and cooled down and ready to serve by now."

"What are we waiting for? Let's go."

Thirty-Six

It felt so good, so familiar, being on the floor, warming up, waiting for the game to start. The championship game. The crowd was buzzing. So was my head. My whole body was tingling. That was the way it always felt before a game. The bigger the game, the bigger the buzz and the stronger the tingle. It wouldn't go away until the first bucket or the first rebound or the first time I pushed against somebody fighting for position.

I dribbled the ball, pulled up and put up my shot. It went in, nothing but net. As Aaron grabbed the rebound, he sent the ball to the next player in the shooting line. I went to the end of the rebounding line. Junior was in front of me.

"Nice shot," he said as I settled in behind him.

"I'm feeling good. It's you I'm worried about. Your last three shots have been bricks."

"You know what they say. Bad warm-up, good game," Junior said.

"If that's true, you're going to have a *great* game."

We shuffled forward in line.

"Big crowd," I noted.

"You know me. The bigger the audience, the better the performance."

"I wish I had your confidence."

"And looks, style, fashion sense and comfortable way of talking to girls. Actually, if you had all of those, you *would* have my confidence."

Before I could answer he went in for the rebound.

I looked up to the end of the gym. My dad, with my mom beside him, stood at the top of the bleachers. I was happy he was here. Maybe even happier that they were standing together again.

The ball went up, and I went in and corralled the rebound. I looked up. It was Tammy in line next, and I passed the ball hard, clear and straight—and right into her hands. As I ran into the next line, I turned to watch her put up her shot. It went rim, backboard, rim, then dropped.

"Nice shot, Tammy!" I yelled.

She answered with a smile. I still loved those smiles. Even if they were coming from a friend instead of a girl-friend. She and I had talked the day before. We'd agreed that we both needed a teammate and friend more than we needed a girlfriend or boyfriend. Maybe in the future things would be different. Who knew what might happen.

The scorekeeper sounded the buzzer. Two minutes left until the start of the game. Coach called us in. We crowded around him.

"Great warm-ups," Coach said. "We're ready for this. I want us to go and have a great first minute, and follow that up with an even better second minute and a nearly perfect third minute."

"We got it, Coach!" Junior yelled. "We got it!"

Everybody cheered.

"We've come a long way," Coach said. "Sometimes we went the wrong way."

We all knew the things he was talking about. Aaron and I locked eyes. He gave me a wink, and I nodded back. He and I were good.

"It isn't about the beginning or the middle. It's about the end. I know we're going to win, no matter what the score is at the end. Nothing but winners here."

The ref blew his whistle, and a roar went out from the crowd as a shot of electricity went up my spine.

"Okay, starters in. Let's do this," Coach said, and we all cheered.

Tammy, Aaron, Junior, Jing and I walked onto the court as everybody else went to the bench.

"No worries. I got this," Junior said.

"*We* got this," Tammy said, correcting him.

He smiled. "We got this."

Jing settled in to take the tip. He was taller than the other center. He knew the play. We all knew the play. He was going to try to tip it forward to me, and I was going to pass to a breaking Aaron.

I looked up to where my parents stood. My dad waved.

With the fingers of my right hand I tapped my chest over my heart twice and pointed up at him. He smiled and did the same back. And right then, standing on the court, I knew it was going to be okay. No matter what happened in the game, I was coming out of this a winner.

The ref tossed the ball up.

Acknowledgments

The writing of a book is usually a dance between the writer and the editor. In this case, it was also between two writers. People often asked if it was a hard process. But to be honest, it was remarkably easy—and fun too. Paul and I talked, wrote, joked, edited and discussed life. Sometimes we couldn't tell where my words stopped and Paul's began, and vice versa. Of course, there are exceptions—any scene involving baking or basketball. I think we all know who wrote those ones.

—Eric

My thanks to Andrew, Tanya and the entire team at Orca Book Publishers for giving this book a home in your house.

To the Canadian children's book community for your support, to my friends and, of course, my family, who never fail to be there.

To Velta and Nick, who I could feel at moments when coincidence wasn't enough to explain how seamlessly things lined up.

And my deepest respect, admiration, and gratitude to Eric. There aren't words or thanks enough. I think we're now officially in a "bromance" so I eagerly await a lesson on the shooting hoops thing I kept reading about in our book.

—Paul

Paul Coccia is the author of *The Player* and the bestselling Orca Soundings title *Cub*, which was a Junior Library Guild Gold Standard Selection. He has an MFA in creative writing from UBC and lives in Toronto with his family.

Eric Walters is a Member of the Order of Canada and the author of over 115 books that have collectively won more than 100 awards, including the Governor General's Literary Award for *The King of Jam Sandwiches*. A former teacher, Eric began writing as a way to get his fifth-grade students interested in reading and writing. Eric is a tireless presenter, speaking to over one hundred thousand students per year in schools across the country. He lives in Guelph, Ontario.